THIS WOMAN IS DEATH

THE CLASSIC HANK JANSON

The first original Hank Janson book appeared in 1946, and the last in 1971. However, the classic era on which we are focusing in the Telos reissue series lasted from 1946 to 1953. The following is a checklist of those books, which were subdivided into five main series and a number of 'specials'.

PRE-SERIES BOOKS
When Dames Get Tough (1946)
Scarred Faces (1947)

SERIES ONE
1) This Woman Is Death (1948)
2) Lady, Mind That Corpse (1948)
3) Gun Moll For Hire (1948)
4) No Regrets For Clara (194)
5) Smart Girls Don't Talk (1949)
6) Lilies For My Lovely (1949)
7) Blonde On The Spot (1949)
8) Honey, Take My Gun (1949)
9) Sweetheart, Here's Your Grave (1949)
10) Gunsmoke In Her Eyes (1949)
11) Angel, Shoot To Kill (1949)
12) Slay-Ride For Cutie (1949)

SERIES TWO
13) Sister, Don't Hate Me (1949)
14) Some Look Better Dead (1950)
15) Sweetie, Hold Me Tight (1950)
16) Torment For Trixie (1950)
17) Don't Dare Me, Sugar (1950)
18) The Lady Has A Scar (1950)
19) The Jane With The Green Eyes (1950)
20) Lola Brought Her Wreath (1950)
21) Lady, Toll The Bell (1950)
22) The Bride Wore Weeds (1950)
23) Don't Mourn Me Toots (1951)
24) This Dame Dies Soon (1951)

SERIES THREE
25) Baby, Don't Dare Squeal (1951)
26) Death Wore A Petticoat (1951)
27) Hotsy, You'll Be Chilled (1951)

28) It's Always Eve That Weeps (1951)
29) Frails Can Be So Tough (1951)
30) Milady Took The Rap (1951)
31) Women Hate Till Death (1951)
32) Broads Don't Scare Easy (1951)
33) Skirts Bring Me Sorrow (1951)
34) Sadie Don't Cry Now (1952)
35) The Filly Wore A Rod (1952)
36) Kill Her If You Can (1952)

SERIES FOUR
37) Murder (1952)
38) Conflict (1952)
39) Tension (1952)
40) Whiplash (1952)
41) Accused (1952)
42) Killer (1952)
43) Suspense (1952)
44) Pursuit (1953)
45) Vengeance (1953)
46) Torment (1953)
47) Amok (1953)
48) Corruption (1953)

SERIES 5
49) Silken Menace (1953)
50) Nyloned Avenger (1953)

SPECIALS
Auctioned (1952)
Persian Pride (1952)
Desert Fury (1953)
One Man In His Time (1953)
Unseen Assassin (1953)
Deadly Mission (1953)

THIS WOMAN IS DEATH

HANK JANSON

This edition first published in the UK in 2013 by
Telos Publishing Ltd,
17 Pendre Avenue, Prestatyn, LL19 9SH,
www.telos.co.uk

Telos Publishing Ltd values feedback. Please e-mail us
with any comments you may have about this book to:
feedback@telos.co.uk

ISBN: 978-1-84583-871-3

Novel by Stephen D Frances
Cover by Reginald Heade
Silhouette device by Philip Mendoza

First published in England by S D Frances, 1948

PUBLISHER'S NOTE

The appeal of the Hank Janson books to a modern readership lies not only in the quality of the storytelling, which is as powerfully compelling today as it was when they were first published, but also in the fascinating insight they afford into the attitudes, customs and morals of the 1940s and 1950s. We have therefore endeavoured to make *This Woman is Death*, and all our other Hank Janson reissues, as faithful to the original editions as possible. Unlike some other publishers, who when reissuing vintage fiction have been known to edit it to remove aspects that might offend present-day sensibilities, we have left the original narrative absolutely intact.

The original editions of these classic Hank Janson titles made quite frequent use of phonetic 'Americanisms' such as 'kinda', 'gotta', 'wanna' and so on. Again, we have left these unchanged in the Telos Publishing Ltd reissues, to give readers as genuine as possible a taste of what it was like to read these books when they first came out, even though such devices have since become sorta out of fashion.

The only way in which we have amended the

original text has been to correct obvious lapses in spelling, grammar and punctuation, and to remedy clear typesetting errors.

Lastly, we should mention that we have made every effort to trace and acquire relevant copyrights in the various elements that make up this book. However, if anyone has any further information that they could provide in this regard, we would be very grateful to receive it.

REISSUE COVER

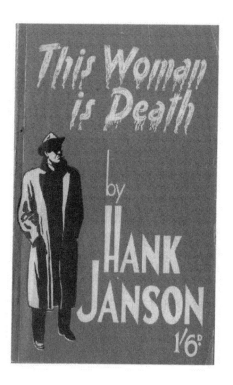

1

There were 20 or so folk lined up at the bar of the Florida when I steered Lola to one of the individually-lighted side tables. She was a sweet kid. I'd known her since she was 12 and wearing pig-tails, and she looked upon me as a big brother.

'What'll it be?' asked the waiter, as he turned on the table lamp and dabbed at imaginary crumbs.

'Two Old-Fashioneds and sandwiches,' I told him. 'Okay with you, Lola?'

'Suits me fine,' she said and began pushing her hair about with the tips of her fingers in the way that women do. She looked right cute, sitting there with her big eyes smiling over towards the bar. I reminded myself again that I'd have to give this big brother stuff the pay-off. I'd been meaning to do so a long time, but being away from home so long hadn't given me a chance to get stuck into the idea.

Lola was cute enough to have lots of fellas playing around in her back garden, although it never got so crowded she couldn't spend an evening with me whenever I got back into town.

'Those guys sure are stewed,' she commented,

nodding her bead towards the bar.

I took a quick gander at them. Judging by the way the bartender sweated, they'd been keeping him busy.

'He sets 'em up; we drink 'em down,' Lola murmured.

'What a job,' I said, thinking of the bartender.

'Yeah. It's hell to live,' she said, and there was bitterness in her voice.

'Isn't that Arden Jnr over there?' I said quickly, to change the conversation. Lola was always bitter about her job. She'd had a fine chance of graduating to college after passing her exams with honours. But just then her father had died and Lola had elected to go out to work to keep her bedridden mother. I reckoned modelling dresses was a job Lola could do ten times better than the next, but deep down inside, she resented having to miss that opportunity. But she kept a stiff upper lip. I doubt if any other person, apart from me, ever guessed how much of a sacrifice she'd made.

'You can't see straight,' she said.

'That's through being dazzled by you.' It was a weak rejoinder, but it changed the line of conversation.

'More likely that blonde over there dazzled you.'

I'm not saying that Lola mightn't have been right. There certainly was an eyeful of blonde perched on a high stool. She had legs, too. From where I was sitting you couldn't doubt she had legs. Those high stools may be uncomfortable to sit on but they have their advantages.

'Hey, remember me?' said Lola.

'Yeah, yeah,' I said, tearing my eyes away from the two points of interest.

'Not that I want to stand in your way, honey,' said Lola. 'But the fella with her looks tough enough to take a swing at competition.'

I guess Lola was right there too. He was a young, fine-built six-footer. You could tell right away that his shoulders weren't all padding. He was some hero. And judging by the way he was looking into the blonde's eyes, he was sure swallowed up on her.

It was just at that moment that the drunk sitting next to the Hero clumsily tipped his glass over so that beer flooded along the bar. It swirled around the Hero's elbow and cascaded into the Blonde's lap.

It all happened so quickly that the damage had been done before anyone realised it.

The Blonde reacted first. She gave a scream, leaped off the stool as though it was red-hot and began dabbing at her lap. She was just about ten times quicker off the mark than her boyfriend. He kinda stared, stupefied, until his sleeve soaked up sufficient moisture to penetrate to his arm, and then he was off his stool with a 'Say, what the hell?'

'Shorry,' said the drunk, waving his arm and nearly sending another glass flying. 'Doan marrew. I'll buy nuther. Nuther drin there.' He banged on the counter. 'Hey, bring me nuther drin, willya?'

The Hero was one of those fellas with an ugly temper. He may have been slow off the mark, but once be got around to figuring things out, he liked to do things thoroughly.

'Say, did you upset that beer?' he asked.

'Doan marrew. Buy nuther. No 'arm, no 'arm.'

'No harm, eh? Just look at this lady's dress.'

'Doan wanna look. Doan worry. Doan like the place, go somewhere else.'

The drunk obviously wasn't himself. Most fellas would have cursed him roundly and left it at that. But the Hero wasn't made that way. It happened so quickly that I didn't realise he was moving fast for a change, until I saw his fingers digging into the drunk's throat.

'Why, you little rat …' he began.

The Blonde got hold of his arm and tried to pull him away; the bartender got his arms in between the two men and began to lever; two or three of the bar-leaners got up so quickly that their stools rocked over backwards; and right in the middle of it the double doors burst open and three grim, menacing figures spread themselves across the entrance.

The Hero didn't see them, but the Blonde did, and the scream she gave was so full of horror that it cut through all the rest of the hubbub. For a moment everything looked like a motion picture still.

The Hero was looking towards the invading gangsters with his mouth slightly open, his fingers still digging into the drunk's throat. The Blonde was cringing back against the counter staring with panic-stricken eyes. The bartender, who I've never before known to be surprised at anything, just gaped.

'All right, Morton,' growled the centre man. 'We want you.' From the way he held his hand in his pocket, I knew he was ready to throw lead. 'Make it snappy, Morton.'

And then the Blonde split the air again. Shriek after shriek, loaded with agonised panic, rang out. I could tell by the way her eyes rolled that she was crazy with fear.

One of the gorillas stepped forward and swung his knotted fist up from the waist. The clop it made as it connected with her jaw sounded like a meat cleaver cutting into a side of beef. The scream was clopped off clean and the Blonde went splaying backwards, landing spreadeagled across her stool.

Everything was happening so quickly that nobody else was moving. You know how it is. Something happens quickly among a large crowd and everybody stands stupid and watches without raising a finger.

The man who'd smacked the Blonde grabbed the Hero's arm and jerked him towards the door, and then the drunk who'd only just got his neck released started hitting out. He swung wildly, but his fist caught the gorilla behind the ear. The gorilla staggered backwards as the drunk, fighting mad, planted a fist in the middle of the Hero's pan.

Then one of the other gorillas got busy. He fired through his pocket, which isn't the best way to aim a gun, and the drunk spun around, twisted by the force of the lead that mashed his hand.

For a moment he gazed stupefied at the blood gouting from the place where his fingers used to be, and then with a mad bull roar he rushed at the lead-slinger.

Another slug tore into him, but he was going pretty fast by that time and his impetus carried him smack onto the killer. The Hero, moving quickly, wasn't far behind him, and the other two toughs got scared and started blazing as well.

It all happened so quickly. Right from the time the beer was spilled until the time the entrance doors swung together behind the killers as they beat it, not more than ten seconds had elapsed. The air was full of smoke, my ears were ringing, the Hero and the drunk were down, two other men were bleeding like pigs all over the bar and Lola was lying splayed across our table and a crimson stain was spreading over the tablecloth in front of me.

2

I just couldn't believe it had happened. One minute we were sitting there, talking and then ... Then Lola was lying across the table, lying there quietly while something inside me was clamouring frantically to make me believe it was all a dream.

I reached out and touched Lola's hand. It was limp. The feel of her was alien. I gagged and heard a voice I knew was mine screaming her name.

'Lola, my god, Lola!'

I took her face between my hands and lifted her head so that I could look into her eyes. But her head was strangely heavy and her cheeks cool and white. I gently rested her head on the table again and felt her pulse – or rather, tried to feel her pulse. And when I couldn't feel it, I went frantic, ripped at her blouse to feel her heartbeat. Instead I found an ugly little red hole in her soft white flesh from which a fine trickle of blood was beginning to run. Another smaller and neater hole in her back showed where the slug had entered.

It happened just like that.

I was dead myself, too. It was as though everything in me stopped working. I couldn't feel. I couldn't think. I was just numb from head to heels. I stood and stared and still couldn't believe that Lola was dead. In some vague way I was conscious of the uproar around me, the shouts of men, the hysterical screams of women, the groans of wounded men, and somewhere outside the shrill screech of police whistles.

And then suddenly I wanted to get out of there. I didn't reason about it. I couldn't think straight anyway. I just felt that I wanted to get away before I went mad; get somewhere quiet where I could lie back and forget, stop thinking, stop feeling numb the way I was feeling.

Unsteadily I walked across the room towards the back door. It didn't seem to matter about leaving Lola there. She wasn't Lola anymore. She was just some poor dame that got shot up in a stick-up party. She wasn't Lola anymore. Not the Lola I knew, who could laugh and dance and hold my hand meaningfully. Behind me, sprawled across the table, was all that was left of Lola. But it wasn't the part of Lola that counted.

A man jostled against me. I pushed him to one side without giving him a second glance. A chair tipped over and fell in front of me and I kicked it to one side. Somebody got hold of my arm and shouted at me. I didn't seem to notice what he was saying and tried to brush him off. But he clung to my arm and shouted and wouldn't let go. It seemed all so senseless and unnecessary. I planted my fist in the middle of his pan and he slipped away out of my sight. Even then he bunched himself around my legs and tried to hold me. I just didn't feel anything or care. I kicked out and my foot clumped against something soft and yielding.

That's just how it was. Like a real dream. And all the time I was just wanting to get out of that place and knowing that there was a back entrance.

The door marked 'Staff Only' seemed to appear before my eyes. I don't know whether I pushed it open or punched it open. And there, right the other side, was the Blonde who had been sitting up at the bar. Only she was a very frightened dame now. There was a wild look in her eyes and she was frantic. I've never seen a dame who looked so scared.

She rushed at me and grabbed me by the arm. It was just like it had been outside. People grabbing at me and shouting. I brushed her off. She grabbed me again and held tight. I placed my palm under her chin and levered, and not too gently at that. She went flying back and hit the ground with a bump, just a flying tangle of filmy underclothes and silk stockings.

I walked on, kinda mechanically I guess, and then a small but firm hand caught my shoulder and somehow managed to twist me around. That same hand slapped me hard across the face. And before I could think, I got three more hard slaps that brought me into focus.

I stood there limply looking at her. My face smarted so that I could still feel each and every finger of her hand. But that slap had been like a douche of cold water.

She was panting a little and her hair was all over her head. There was still that stark panic in her eyes.

'Look, mister,' she said. ' I'm sorry I had to do that, but I gotta get out of here.'

I was beginning to live again. The smart of my face was real, the things around me were real and the Blonde was real. I was even able to think again.

'What's holding you back?' I said.

'You know this joint. Gemme out, willya?'

'Back door.' I jerked my head in that direction.

'That's no good,' she said. 'There's 20,000

rubbernecks outside.'

That made me think quickly.

'Think of something, willya,' she mouthed at me. 'And don't go crazy on me again, unless you want another slap.'

But I wasn't going crazy again. That slap had brought me back to my senses. I was remembering things. And I wasn't just remembering Lola sprawled over the table. I was remembering this Blonde's face when those three gorillas came in. I remembered how she'd screamed and how she'd recognised them before any shooting started. And I knew right then that if there was any way to find the men who'd done for Lola, it was through this Blonde.

'Okay, sister,' I said, 'follow me.'

I ran along the passage towards the back staircase. Her heels clip-clopped along behind me, and I found time to wonder that she could keep pace with me in those high-heeled shoes.

I ran up the stairs two at a time. At the end of the first flight she was still right behind me.

'Is this a gag?' she yelled. ' I wanna get out, not up.'

I didn't answer and she followed me like I knew she would.

On the third floor I walked rapidly along the corridor to the end where the Gents' toilet was. I opened the door and she kinda teetered on the threshold.

'Get in, willya,' I said and gave her a shove. There was probably all kinds of ideas chasing around in her head, but she relaxed when I levered back the catch and opened the window.

I looked out and she pushed alongside me. I could smell the scent of her hair and she was using some delicate and expensive perfume. For the first time since she'd got me by the arm downstairs I realised that she was a dame and an attractive dame at that ...

'See that parapet there?' I pointed down to a sloping roof about 12 feet beneath us. It was fringed by a wide, three feet parapet that ran along the rooftops for a good few blocks .

'I can't make it,' she said, and there was a tremble in her voice.

'Listen, lady, if you can't make it, here's where you and me part company.' I swung one leg over the sill and she grabbed me by the arm.

'You'll have to help me,' she said.

'All you do, Blondie, is hang by your arms and drop. Only you've got to drop careful, because if you miss your footing you'll likely roll over the edge.'

She shuddered. 'I can't do it,' she moaned. She was trembling all over.

I looked around me. The cistern chain was long and strong. I unhooked it from its arm. It wasn't long enough by half. But Blondie had an answer for that. For the second time in less than five minutes her skirts were way up above her knees. She was fumbling among a creamy froth of underclothes, loosening suspenders and peeling off skin-tight nylons.

I drew a deep breath.

'Lady, you can book me for a front seat every night you care to repeat that performance.'

'Hold that,' she said, thrusting one of the stockings in my hand, while she knotted the other to it. I could still feel her warmth ensnared in the fine threads. I liked the feel of it.

She gave a tug to test the strength of our improvised rope. It held good and strong.

'Now your belt,' she snapped.

It was funny how she'd changed and become all efficient. I watched her fingers deftly securing the stockings to the buckle of my belt. She gave another tug to test its strength.

'That'll do.'

She stuck her head out of the window and looked down, and all at once she swayed. I saw her knuckles clenched tightly on the sill.

'There's nothing to it,' I said.

She shuddered again. 'I can't do it,' she whispered. 'I can't stand heights.'

It was my turn to slap her face. I didn't hold anything in reserve, and her head snapped back with a click. While she was still trying to think that over, I wound one end of the stockings around her wrist and tied it tightly.

There wasn't much time to lose. Somewhere downstairs I could hear the clamour of voices and the tramping of boots. Somehow I bundled her over the sill, and then all at once she was dangling by one arm. I lowered away.

I hated to think what that stocking was doing to her wrist. Every nerve in her arm must have been shrieking in agony. When she was halfway down, she was so quiet I realised she must have passed out. No dame could have stood that much pain without squawking. That made it more difficult, because I still had to get down myself and I daren't release my end of the rope, because she'd roll.

And sure enough she did roll. I held tight to my end, and there she was lying half across the gutter with only the nylon around her wrist saving her from a 60-foot dive onto asphalt.

Fortunately it was one of those windows with sashes. I jammed the lower sash down hard and it held my end of the chain firmer than I could have held it myself. Then I pulled the upper sash right down as far as it would go. Then I climbed over the top of both sashes and lowered myself over the sill. For a few sickly seconds I hung by my fingertips before I breathed a prayer and let go. The next moment my feet hit the roof beneath and I was skidding and sliding, clawing frantically at the slates with my fingernails.

My foot lodging in the gutter saved me. I lay spreadeagled for some moments, getting back my wind and my confidence, and then I crawled along to Blondie. She was still out cold, which wasn't very helpful but may have been the best way for her to be at the moment. I eased her back from over the gutter, wedged her so she shouldn't start sliding and untied the stocking from the end of my belt. I still left one end of the stocking tied around her wrist, because we weren't through yet.

It may sound easy to talk about crawling over a sloping roof, but anyone that's tried knows how tricky it is. I know I found it difficult – and I wasn't chancing anything. I crawled along as far as the length of stocking allowed, lay flat on my belly, dug in hard with toes and elbows and then pulled Blondie after me. By the time I got to the parapet she was just coming around.

She moaned a bit.

'Take it easy, honey,' I said.

Her eyes flickered open and she looked like she'd never seen me before. Then her eyes flicked down to her wrist.

She didn't even whimper as I untied the stocking. It was difficult to get undone, because it was all mixed up with bits of loose skin and blood.

'That doesn't look pretty,' she said, and I saw her small white teeth biting into her lip.

'Maybe not,' I said, 'but it looks a lot healthier than a big red smear on a white asphalt pavement.'

I gave her a few minutes' rest and then stood up. She got up, too, pretty shaky.

I led the way, and I knew where I was going. During prohibition, when the Florida had been a speakeasy, I'd used this exit a good many times.

The parapet finished at the end of the block. A fire-escape ran down the outside of the building to a narrow courtyard. Five minutes later we were on firm ground again.

3

For the first time, we were able to take a breather. Blondie sure needed it, too. And she looked a mess. Somehow in that wild scramble across the rooftops, she'd ripped her skirt so that it bared her leg, revealing a flimsy wisp of panties. A black smear of dirt ran across her cheek and across her forehead, and the handkerchief she'd tied around her wrist was already soaked with blood.

She caught my eye and pinched together the tear in her skirt. 'Got a pin?'

I found one tucked in the lapel of my jacket. 'You'll need more than a pin to put you right,' I said.

'I'll say.' She held up one foot, and for the first time I noticed she'd lost a shoe.

'Where's it gone?'

She shrugged. 'Back there somewhere.'

'Can't go back for it,' I said. I looked around. The courtyard was quite deserted. ' Just hold on here till I grab my car,' I instructed.

'Make it snappy,' she said. 'I don't want any Nosey Parkers trying to get fresh!'

I brushed down my clothes quickly, wiped my

face and hands with my pocket handkerchief and casually strolled out into the main drag. My car was parked two blocks down.

Even as I was getting into the driving seat, another squad of cops sirened past. I gripped the steering wheel tightly and a momentary cold chill crept down my spine as I thought again of Lola. So much had happened and all of it so quickly that it was still hard to believe. A cold fury began to mount inside me. I slashed in the gears and stepped on the gas. I felt I just wanted to rend and tear – only there was nobody I could take it out on – yet.

I pulled up at the entrance to the courtyard. At first I got a shock, because I thought Blondie had scrammed. But there she was, pressed up tight against the wall and standing on one foot. She'd cleaned up a bit, too, and it made me go soft to see her standing there, such a pathetic figure with five bare little toes delicately poised off the ground.

'Take my arm,' I said. 'And get in the car as quickly as you can. Don't start waving your bare toes around. Some bum dick may have grabbed that shoe and might connect up.'

'I'm not dumb,' she said.

She held my arm tightly. Partly, I guess, because it's difficult to hobble with one foot on firm ground while the other is in a six-inch heeled shoe. Partly, I hoped, because she wanted it that way.

I bundled her in the car, whipped around to the other door, slid inside and let up the clutch.

'Where to, lady?'

'Eh?' she seemed startled – thoughtful.

'Jeezus, don't you know where you live?'

All the panic and fear I'd seen before brimmed

up into her eyes.

'Yon can't take me home,' she said.

'Listen, lady, I'm no wolf. You've gotta go home. Where else can you get a wash and a change of clothes?'

She began fumbling at the door handle on her side. It was just crazy. We were doing 30 by this time – even in the city limits.

I reached across and smacked her hand down.

'Are you crazy?' I demanded.

'You've gotta let me out,' she said.

'Do I smell?' I spoke from the corner of my mouth, my eye on the road.

'You can't take me home.'

I became impatient. 'Listen, Blondie. I don't care where the hell you go. But you need a change, and that hand wants a bandage. If your old man doesn't like strangers, I'll drop you at the gate and disappear.'

She was thoughtful. 'All right,' she said at last. 'Take me to Seventh Avenue, 143rd.'

That was away across town. I turned off right and set our nose heading that way.

'That bandage,' she said. 'Better stop at a drug store and get a supply. Got a cigarette?'

I fumbled and produced a packet. She took the packet from me. The traffic was thick at that point. She lit mine for me and thrust it between my lips. The taste of her lipstick spoilt the cigarette, but it was an intimate kinda thing to do and I liked her doing it.

I braked at a drug store.

'Get me a packet of headache pills as well,' she instructed.

I nodded, crossed over the road and waited while an old white-coated dodderer behind the counter laboriously climbed a ladder to the top shelves for a prescription mixture for somebody else.

It took me all of ten minutes to get outa that shop. I crossed back over the road and then stood stock still. Blondie was gone. But my car was gone, too, and that made me really mad.

4

'What's the matter, bud?'

It was a cabbie, who'd seen me glaring furiously up and down the street.

'A friend's taken my car for a joke,' I said.

His indicator showed he was free. 'Take a cruise,' I instructed. 'Green Chevrolet, 761313. Lady driver.'

'Any idea which way?'

'Try 143rd Street.' I knew that would be a phoney address, but he may as well drive that way as any other.

'Some fellows get tough and tell the cops when their cars get pinched,' said the cabbie.

'Some fellas mind their own business,' I said.

'Okay, pal. Have it your way.'

He cruised along a block or two and then said:

'Seems there was trouble way down on Fifteenth, the Florida.'

'Yeah?' I grunted.

'Yeah,' he said. 'A battalion of cops was there when I passed. Seems like some tough guys slung lead around. A fare I just dropped says there were ten stiffs and a score or so of wounded, including about a dozen dames.'

'Some yarns get stretched,' I said.

'I don't make no statements, bud. That's what I heard.'

'Hear anything else?'

'Nuthin' important.'

'Hear who the fellas were, for example?'

'Hearing's one thing. Telling's another.'

'I've just got a bump of curiosity,' I said.

'Some folks with one of them things wind up in morgues.'

'Some get an extra five bucks when they drop their passengers.'

He thought that over awhile.

'Ya wouldn't be stringing a fella along, would ya?'

'Listen pal, I'm a reporter. News is my business.'

'Write a stick on what it's like to have ya car pinched,' he suggested.

'Night editors prefer the lowdown on killings,' I said.

He went on thinking it over for a bit. 'Did ya say ten bucks?' he asked.

'Ten bucks is yours, brother, if I get what I want.'

He still hesitated. Then ... 'Mind, this is only what I heard ...'

'Yeah, yeah,' I broke in. 'You heard it from some bird who heard it from some dame who heard it from another fella. Just spill it, brother. I won't hold it against you.'

'Some guys seem to think it may have been Nat Garvin's hoods.'

'And who the heck is Nat Garvin?' I asked.

The question seemed to freeze him for a moment. Then he turned and stared at me.

'Smart guy,' he said.

'Just dumb,' I said.

He looked around in time to avoid a tram. After he'd swerved violently and righted the cab again, he said, out of the corner of his mouth:

'Newspaper fellas know their way around.'

'I'm new,' I said. 'That's why I ask questions.'

He chewed that over for a while. In fact he chewed it over and tossed it around in his mouth for quite a while before he swallowed it.

'Nat Garvin's an operator,' he said. 'Runs the numbers racket, pin table saloons, owns a dozen or so nightclubs and runs a fleet of taxis. Brother, he's big in this town.'

'Where's he hang out? I asked.

'Take a tip from me, buddy. Nat ain't the kinda guy one fools around with asking questions for the morning news. The Golden Peacock is where he sets most evenings. But only his pals or guys with tough stomachs get around to interviews.'

He seemed to shrink into himself after that. We drove around a block or two, but it was like looking for a single needle in a score of haystacks. I decided to leave it for a night and see what turned up.

'Turn it up, buddy,' I said. 'Take me back to Fifth Avenue.'

5

It was midnight before I got any further forward. I'd eaten, bathed and smoked 40 or so cigarettes. The butts were scattered around the floor where I'd thrown them down, half-smoked and ground out with my heel.

I'd downed almost a full bottle of Scotch without it making the slightest impression on me. You see, Lola had got under my skin. She was all I could think about. Lola lying there with that little hole drilled through her white breast. I thought of her, how bravely she'd tackled life. And I thought of her crippled Ma, unable to work and wondering where Lola was.

I hadn't the guts to go around and tell her Ma, and that's straight. I took the easy way out and knew nothing. Which was a lousy thing to do. But all I could do was to stride up and down the room, thinking of Lola and planning how I'd make those gunmen suffer for what they'd done.

I don't think I was quite sane, because nobody could go through all I'd suffered that day and still be sane.

It was just on midnight when the phone rang. I scrunched another cigarette on the floor and grabbed the phone.

'Yeah,' I bawled.

'Name of Janson?'

'So what?'

'Police headquarters here. You gotta car 761313?'

'That's my heap.'

'What's it doing parked out on Madison Square? Been there three hours without lights.'

I calmed down a bit. 'That's my car,' I said. 'Some bum stole it from the park this afternoon. I've been waiting for a call.'

'Did you notify the police?'

'No,' I said. 'No ... I ... er ...'

'That's a bit thin, brother,' said the voice. 'Guess you'd better collect it right away. We got better things to do than act as car watchers for forgetful guys. You'll be hearing from us later.'

He hung up.

Well, that was that. Blondie had dumped my car. There was nothing else for it but to get the car and try and trace Blondie some way, somehow.

That was the rub. Blondie knew for sure who those gunmen were. But I had to find Blondie before I could get that information. And Blondie seemed kinda shy.

But it wasn't until after I'd collected the heap and parked it around the back that I got my first lead on that dame.

Usually I keep the key of the garage in the cubby hole on the dashboard. As I fumbled there I felt something soft and clinging. I pulled it out. It was the stocking Blondie had been wearing. Not much of a clue, but it might lead to something.

I took it upstairs with me, lit another cigarette, poured myself a strong dose of Scotch and examined the stocking with minute care. The only thing on the stocking was the name 'Nylonlite.' It was on a tab sewn into the top of the stocking.

Just what it meant beyond being a trade name I didn't know. But I meant to find out.

So the next morning I duly presented myself to Madame Louise.

It's one of those joints frequented by women only. I walked in there staring straight in front of me, trying not to see the corseted, strapped up dummies, the brassiered wax models and the almost indignant stares of feminine customers who plucked with sensitive fingers at flimsy underclothes of all descriptions and in all shades.

With red cheeks and hot, sweating palms I arrived at the stocking counter.

Under the glass counter were displayed hundreds of pairs of sheer silk stockings. A dozen or more delicately-poised glass legs advertised the transparent glory of pure silken sheaths. A big placard garlanded with stockings hung over the counter and announced 'STOCKINGS.'

A condescending, self-confident young woman, dressed smartly, swept me into her orbit.

'Good morning, sir. Is there anything I can get for you?'

My cheeks got redder, my hands more sweaty, and I stammered awkwardly.

'Do … er … er … do you sell stockings?'

I felt a punk. And my question made me into a pink, blushing punk. The girl just smiled precisely and said:

'Yes, sir. We do sell stockings. What size do you want?'

I wasn't getting far that way. So I pulled the

stocking from my pocket and displayed the name tab.

'D'you sell these?' I asked.

She glanced casually at the name tab. 'Naturally. We stock all the best brands.'

I gulped and took the plunge.

'I'm a dick, see? Trying to trace the owner of these.'

'Oh!' For the first time the girl became human. I'd startled her. I followed up my advantage.

'I want to trace the girl who bought these. What can you tell me?'

She took the stocking from me and turned it over in her white hands. I saw her mouth form a small O as she saw the bloodstains.

'Was it a murder?' she whispered.

'Yeah,' I said. 'Pretty serious affair. What can you tell me?'

She turned the stockings over and over in her hands. I stood there waiting, breathless. At last the dame looked at me.

'I'm afraid I can't help. Anyone can buy these stockings anywhere in town. Nearly every shop will stock this brand and there's no way of telling which store they came from.'

Well. That was that. I'd got a blind lead.

I dropped the stocking in the gutter and trailed along the pavement thinking what I could do next. I thought about Lola again and I boiled all over. Then I thought about Blondie. I remembered her climbing over those rooftops. I remembered how we'd climbed down the fire-escape, I remembered how I'd gone to get my car and come back for her, and I remembered how she'd been waiting there, balanced on one foot.

Balanced on one foot!

D'you get it? She'd lost a shoe on those rooftops.

Back I went to the Florida. I hung around for a bit to make sure the cops were giving it a clear berth, then I went in.

First thing I did when I got inside was to look across to where Lola and I had been sitting. Somehow I thought I might still see her sprawled across the table.

But some big, fat guy was sitting there with a napkin tucked in his collar. Everything was busy and businesslike. You wouldn't have thought that 24 hours previously a gang of hoodlums had been shooting up the joint.

I sauntered through to the back, stood there a moment making play I was lighting a cigarette, and then, when nobody was looking, I slipped through the 'Staff' door.

Up the stairs I went, along the corridor to the Gents' toilet. The lavatory chain had been refixed, I noticed as I went through, and when I lifted up the sash and looked out of the window I saw what I wanted. Lying in the gutter was a shoe. It was Blondie's shoe, right enough. That heel was at least six inches high.

6

THE dame behind the counter turned the shoe over carefully in her hand.

'It's one of our shoes,' she commented. 'But I don't think we can say who bought it.'

'Look, Miss,' I said. 'I've already been to eight other branches in this city. There's only nine all told, and this is the ninth. None of the others has sold this model with six-inch heels during the past month, and if you take a good squint at these you'll see they're almost new. Somebody must have sold these shoes.'

She sniffed. 'I suppose so, but we're here to sell shoes, not to spend time turning up records and ...'

'Cut the cackle, lady,' I said, with an edge in my voice. 'I'm wanting information, see. I'll get it here or I'll get it at headquarters. I'll get it either way. But if I get it now, snappy, it'll save you a load of grief.'

'I'll have to ask the manageress ...'

'Ask Father Christmas if you like, but get me that dope quick, willya?'

I snarled at her this time and looked ugly and that scared her a bit. She disappeared behind some ornate curtains, and a few minutes later she was back with a ledger.

She ran her finger down the pages and then she caught her breath.

'Got it?'

She nodded and spun the ledger around. 'Specially made,' she said.

'Would this be the shoe?'

'That's it,' she said.

I took a note of the address, re-wrapped the shoe and thrust it in my pocket.

'Thanks for the information, lady.' I said. 'Next time, answer up a bit more lively or you may get an obstruction charge chalked up against you.'

'You can't scare me, copper,' she said.

I stood back and looked her up and down. I looked at the curve of her hips, then my eyes slowly travelled up, resting lingeringly on the low-cut neckline of her dress, exploring her shoulders and neck and finally resting on her face, which by this time had become flushed with embarrassment.

'I'd like to take you up on that,' I said.

'If you've finished ...'

'I know, you've got work to do. But I still think I can scare you.'

She tossed her head and turned away. I chuckled and walked out.

The address I'd got was a hotel address.

I walked straight through to the receptionist. He was a smart, efficient-looking fella.

'Miss Anvers in?'

He turned and looked at the key rack.

'Nope,' he said.

'Okay, I'll wait. What's her room number?'

'You can wait in the lounge, buddy.'

'I can and will. But just the same, what's her room number.'

'Sixty-nine, if it makes you any happier to know.'

'Call me when she comes.'

He made a note of my name and I sat in the lounge, where I could see who came in, and ordered a Scotch.

I waited a half-hour and still no Blondie. The fella at the reception desk glanced at the clock and beckoned a small page boy who was hovering around. The page boy perched himself behind the counter and off went the receptionist.

I strolled over to the counter.

'Big job this, for a little fella,' I said.

He glared at me ferociously. 'I ain't so little,' he growled.

'Warming the other fella's seat?'

'Yeah,' he grumbled. 'He goes out for a break, but I don't get time out.'

'Lemme have my key, sonny.'

'You a resident? '

'Would I ask for a key otherwise?'

'Guess not. What's your number?'

'Sixty-nine,' I said.

He got it down and laid it on the counter. His hand was moving toward the guest's book to check the name.

'I suppose the other fella gets all the best tips, too.'

'Yeah, he sure does.' His hand was touching the book.

'Well,' I drawled. He looked up at the meaning in my voice. 'I guess a good kid like you will go a long way. You won't get bad breaks all the time. Suppose I gave you a dollar, what'ya do with it?'

He forgot about the book, he forgot about checking

the name. He was just staring at the dollar bill I was holding up.

'Gee, mister,' he said.

'I guess you'd know what to do with it okay,' I said.

'I sure would, mister.'

I flipped the bill across the desk, picked up the keys and dropped them into my pocket very casually.

'When you own your own hotel,' I told him, 'I'll expect you to give me a free lunch.'

'That's a promise, mister.'

I left him carefully tucking away the bill and walked up the stairs. Suite 69 was on the third floor. I opened the door and looked around quickly. It was a typical dame's room, all frills and lace, with thick fancy carpets and lampshades and all that paraphernalia. I walked around the room and picked up a photograph. It showed a dark-haired girl looking out of the frame with a wistful smile fleeting across her face. I wondered who it was. Then across the room I saw another photo. It was Blondie right enough. I crossed back to the door and wedged it so it wouldn't close behind me as I went out.

When I got downstairs, the page boy was still perched on the stool. I tossed him the keys and sauntered back into the lounge. A few minutes later I sauntered out again. He just glanced up from the book he was reading, and when he saw I wasn't looking for him he looked down again.

I went quietly up the stairs, back to suite 69, and let myself in.

It was a swell apartment at that. I wondered how Blondie earned her dough. It needed plenty to keep that joint going.

There were a coupla doors leading off. One led to a

kitchenette, the other to a corridor where the bedroom and the bathroom were.

I wandered around, picking up this thing and that, but there didn't seem to be any signs of a man's occupation around. No pipes, no men's clothes in the wardrobe. Blondie lived alone, I figured.

There was one of those glass cocktail cabinets that opens up like a shop counter when you pull a lever. I mixed myself a highball and settled down in a chair and waited.

It was three cigarettes and two highballs later that I heard the key in the lock. Swiftly I got behind the door as it opened. And as she came in I sidled swiftly behind her and shut the door and rested my back against it.

The dame spun around and gave a gasp of surprise.

I just gaped. This dame wasn't Blondie. She was the other dame whose photograph I'd seen in the flat.

She backed away from me warily.

'Who are you. What are you doing in here?'

She was all het up, ready to scream blue murder and bring the hotel down around my ears.

'Now take it easy, lady,' I said pacifically. 'There's been a mistake.' Involuntarily I stepped towards her. She jumped back two paces and got hold of a chair.

'Easy, easy, now,' I wagged a chiding finger.

'Who let you in? What are you doing here?'

'I just dropped in to see my friend, Blondie … er … the dame whose photograph is on that sideboard.'

Her eyes became hard and her voice brittle.

'What d'you want her for?'

'I just called in to have a chat.'

The suspicion in her eyes intensified.

'D'you come from Garvin?'

'I ... er ... er. Well, yeah, I do.'

I'd said the wrong thing. The dame showed more strength than I thought she had. With a sudden movement she slung the chair at me, and at the same time she dived for the phone.

The chair cracked against my shins. But that didn't worry me so much then. I knew what a short time it took to get a police call through and I didn't waste time. I dived too. We both reached the phone at the same time, only I was on top of her. The phone crashed on the floor and we rolled on the carpet. Like an eel she wriggled from under me. I reached out and cradled the telephone on its rest. Meantime she'd slipped off her shoe.

The heel thudded down on my scalp, sending a shower of sparks fluttering across my eyeballs.

'Hold it, you damn fool ...' I yelled.

The heel thudded down twice more and then I lost my temper. I reached out blindly and clutched a pair of silk-clad legs. I tugged and there was a bump. The next moment the heel missed my eye by an inch and split open my forehead.

At this rate she'd have had me cold in a few minutes.

I caught her down-swinging arm next time and began to twist the shoe from her hand. She swivelled around and sank her teeth in my wrist. At the same time, her other hand clawed at my face. I felt the skin being torn off my cheeks by long, raking fingernails.

That was when I really saw red.

I reached out and grabbed with my free hand and wrenched her over backwards. She twisted so my hand slipped, but her jaws still clamped into my wrist. I clutched at the collar of her dress and pulled and twisted so that the edge of the dress cut into her throat. But the dressmaker hadn't reckoned on that kind of treatment. The dress tore in a V that reached to her waist. Her fingers began to gouge at my eyes.

'You've asked for it,' I muttered, throwing my full weight across the top of her, imprisoning the hand that had been clawing my face.

Tears were spurting out of my eyes now with the pain of my wrist. Her teeth must have been nearly through to the bone. I bent my head over her neck and got my teeth on the lobe of her ear. I've got two very firm and pointed front teeth. I bit hard and I meant to bite hard. I fell my teeth meet.

As she opened her mouth to scream, I wrenched my arm free and clamped it over her mouth. She gave a shudder of pain that ran right through her. I grabbed her by the hair and lifted her head and rammed it back hard against the carpet, then I got two thumbs on her windpipe and squeezed.

All she could think about then was grabbing me by the wrists and trying to stop me from choking her.

I held her that way for a few moments and then eased off.

She opened her mouth to scream again and I increased the pressure suddenly.

'Ya gonna scream again?' I asked.

She lay quiet then and looked up at me with large, terrified eyes.

'If I let ya go, will ya scream again?'

She weakly shook her head and I let go her throat.

She gulped and rubbed her neck. I was still spreadeagled across her and the blood from my cheek was dripping slowly onto the white flesh of her bosom, which peeked through the rent in her dress. Her body felt warm and quivery beneath me.

I thoughtfully sucked my wrist.

'You asked for what ya got, lady.'

She didn't answer. She just stared at me and breathed hard. Then she got her wrists against my chest and thrust me away. I obligingly gave way and sat on the floor, alternatively licking my wrist and mopping at my cheek.

She sat up and smoothed down her skirt.

'You brute,' she said, and there were tears at the corners of her eyes.

'I didn't like that anymore than you. But you don't give a fella a chance to talk.'

She stood up gingerly and balanced on one foot. Then she passed one hand wearily across her forehead.

'My shoe,' she said in a tired voice.

I was still sat on the floor. I looked around and saw her shoe a yard from me. I reached out for it, and as I turned to hand it to her, her swinging foot caught me right across the nose. My head bounced back on the floor and then she jumped on me with both feet right where she guessed it would hurt most. I jack-knifed in agony, sobbing for breath. Everything was spinning around. A shadowy something leaped down at me and I raised my arm to ward it off. My arm went numb from wrist to shoulder. I squinted up quickly. The dame had grabbed a lamp-standard and it was swinging at my head again. I rolled and it hit the floor beside me. I doubled up my knees and kicked out with both feet, knocking her legs from beneath her. For the second time in five minutes she sat on her fanny with a bump. Only this time it was different. I'd had enough of this dame's tough tactics. I got a fistful of hair and jerked her head back. I wrapped both legs around her in the scissors hold and with my free arm fumbled for the flex attached to the lamp-standard.

She began to scream then, so I hooked my arm around her neck and squeezed. That stopped the squawking.

She sure was a scrapper. It took me all my time to get that flex around her wrists and pulled tight behind her back. The moment I eased up on her she began to scream, and there was nothing for it but to run one end of the flex around her throat and down her back to her hands. After that, every time she tried to pull her hands loose she was in danger of choking herself. Even when she didn't try, she was pretty near choking anyway.

I let her stew in her own juice and fumbled my way to the bathroom. Jeez, what that dame had done to me!

It was like looking at a stranger to see my reflection. Blood was oozing from my eyebrow where the heel had caught me, blood from my nose had dripped all over my shirt and masked the lower part of my face and deep scratches furrowed my cheek from brow to chin.

I stripped off my collar and tie and doused my head under the tap, feeling water washing the blood away. Then I doctored myself up with some sticking plaster I found in a medicine cabinet and looked more like a human being.

When I got back to the other room the dame was lying just as I left her, with her skirts up around her waist and exhibiting two excellent arguments in favour of swimsuits. Her face was a dark shade of purple. I thought I'd left her too long at first and my heart gave a jump, but she opened her eyes as I stood over her and she looked at me appealingly and made soft gurgling noises.

'Listen, sister, I'm gonna release you from that stranglehold, see. But if you give one yelp you'll get this ...' I gave her a slap across the face that made my hand sting. 'See what I mean? Now one squeal and you'll get that, only it'll be about ten times as hard. Savvy?'

She tried to nod her head.

'You and me are gonna talk, lady. Nice and quiet, though.' I loosened the flex around her throat and held it in my hand, ready to tug tight again. Then I pulled up a chair, sat down and lit a cigarette.

When her face regained its normal colour I said:

'Where's Blondie?'

'Find out,' she snapped. 'I'm not telling a thing.'

'I'll find out.'

This dame was tough. She'd asked for all she was getting. I pulled the flex tight again and jabbed the end of my cigarette against her thigh, just above the top of her stocking.

I didn't hold the cigarette, I just dabbed it, quickly. Even so, it was as well I wasn't holding the flex too tightly, otherwise she might have cut her head off, the way she jumped.

I gave her a few minutes to think that out, then let up on the flex again. There was no doubt about the tears this time. What with the powder and rouge, her face was looking a mess. I was beginning to feel a heel, too, because she looked such a nice kid. She had guts, too.

'Listen, sister. I hate this as much as you. Why don't you play ball?'

'I don't play ball with Nat Garvin's hoods.'

'Okay. I'll give it to you straight. I don't know Nat Garvin. Never seen him. I'm just wanting to see Blondie on account of a little information she can give me.'

'Don't give me that.'

' Look,' I said earnestly. 'When I came here, I expected to see Blondie. You turned up instead. Now if you'd been a sensible dame and talked this over with me, we'd have got somewhere. Instead you have to start a rough-house. I don't like treating dames this way. But, Jeezus, you've asked for it. Now will ya gimme it straight? Where's Blondie?'

'I don't know,' she said sullenly.

I pulled the flex gently, so that it tightened.

Her eyes flashed angrily.

'Go ahead,' she said. 'Cut me to pieces if you like. But I can't tell what I don't know. I'm giving it straight now,'

I pulled the flex tight. She clenched her teeth into her lip, and her body arched. I brought the cigarette near to where I'd dabbed before, and watched her. She closed her eyes in resignation, and every line of her body quivered in dread anticipation.

I loosened the flex.

'Okay,' I said. 'I believe you.'

She breathed a sigh of relief. 'I could do with a drink,' she muttered.

'Yeah, so you can scream your head off when my back's turned.'

'I need a drink bad. Choke me again if you like, but give me a drink, will you?'

I gave her a long look. 'I'll take a chance on you, sister, but Jeezus, if you let out even the teeniest yelp, I'll give you the whole works.'

I got her a drink. And she didn't yelp. Her eyes followed my every movement as I mixed a strong Scotch for her and another for myself.

I had to put my arm around her and hold the glass to her lips. Being like that made me realise for the first time that she was a cuddlable sorta dame. She had a good figure, too – what was left of her dress after our rough and tumble hadn't left much to the imagination.

'Feel better?'

'Yeah. I'd feel even better if my hands were loose.'

'So'd I. But you might get tough again.'

'If I pass out on you, remember I gave you warning. This wire's just about cutting my wrists in two.'

'I wish I could trust you.'

'Why don't you just blow out of here and let me suffer in peace.'

'I want Blondie,' I said.

She looked up to heaven. 'Get another record.'

'Well ... how does Blondie tie up with you?'

Her eyes were cold. 'Don't kid me. You know that's my sister.'

I remembered the shoe then and lugged it out of my pocket.

'Ever seen this before?'

She looked at it and her eyes widened. 'That's mine. What are you doing with it?'

'What was Blondie doing with it?'

She looked at me wonderingly and then her expression changed and I could almost see her thoughts clicking into position.

'Say, where did you get that shoe?'

'Would you be surprised if I told you I found it in the roof-gutter over by the Florida.'

'They you're ...' she began.

'Yeah, I'm what?' I encouraged.

'No. You tell me, then I'll know if you're lying.'

'Fair enough. I went back for it after I'd lugged Blondie out of the Florida and across the rooftops to get her away from the cops.'

'Then you're not one of Garvin's hoods?'

'Ain't that what I've been telling you?'

'Yeah ... but I thought you'd come for her and ...'

'And?' I encouraged.

'Look,' she said. 'Lemme loose, will you? I'm on the level with you now. I thought you were one of those hoods. Give me a break and I'll explain everything to you.'

I looked at her long and calculatingly.

'I'm on the level,' she pleaded. 'The key of the door is in my handbag. You can cut the phone wires if you like. You can clout me down if I try to scream or anything funny. But for God's sake release my hands, will you? This wire's killing me.'

I looked at her long and lingeringly, weighing it up in my mind.

'Okay,' I said. 'But if you try one smart alec move ...'

7

She hadn't been kidding about that wire. It had cut so deep into the flesh that it couldn't be seen. And when the circulation began to restore itself she almost passed out.

I sat there holding a slug of Scotch in my hand, feeding her with it in sips and feeling a low-down heel each time she gave a moan.

'I'll be all right in a minute,' she said.

I hoped so. But she wasn't looking so good.

'Kinda silly of me,' she said. 'I oughtn't weaken up on you like this.'

'You're doing swell, kid,' I told her.

She tried to smile but it changed into a grimace. I held the glass to her lips and she took a good nip.

Sure enough, after a few minutes the colour came back to her cheeks and, woman-like, the first thing she thought of was her looks.

'I guess I look a sight. Give me a minute to straighten up, will you?'

'Reckon I'll come and hold your hand.'

She grinned at me. Yeah, after all she'd been through, she grinned at me. 'Still don't trust me, eh?'

'It don't pay to take chances.'

'As you like.'

When she looked at herself in the bathroom mirror, she gave a little gasp. 'Hell, what a mess.'

She ran water in the washbasin and cleaned up her puss.

I perched on the edge of the bath, smoking and watching her as she rouged her cheeks and put colour on her lips.

'How come Blondie had your shoes?' I asked.

'Sisters do that kind of thing. Lend shoes, I mean.'

'And she told you about the trouble at the Florida?'

'She did.'

There was something special about the way she said that.

'What d'you mean, by saying it like that?'

She was blacking her eyebrows now, making funny little grimaces to help her along.

'Why do you want to see Blondie?' she asked, avoiding my question.

I thought that over and gave her the straight dope.

'A friend was with me in the Florida. She was a kid about your age. She was a nice kid. I didn't like it when she got a slug in her back. And when I find the fella responsible for it, he ain't gonna be happy either.'

'What's that got to do with Suzy?'

'She knows who did it,' I said.

'Nat Garvin's hoods,' she said meditatively.

'So it *was* his gang.'

'It was him all right. But just you try and hang it on him. He'll have an alibi right enough, and the hoods that did it are well under cover.'

She took it all so calmly that it was a little startling. She didn't look the kinda dame to be mixed up in this kinda trouble .

50

'How come you know so much about it?'

'Being Suzy's sister.' She began to comb her hair and I noticed how it rippled through the comb and shone with a lustre of its own.

'Is she mixed up with them?'

She stopped combing and her voice became serious. 'She can't help herself. That man Garvin's carrying a torch for her that'd set Niagara Falls afire. He just won't leave her alone. She daren't speak to another fella without signing his death warrant.'

'How come?'

She shrugged her shoulders. 'That's the way it is. If Suzy takes a night out with some Romeo, the fella gets bumped off the next day. That's what happened down at the Florida. You saw it happen.'

That knocked me flat. 'You mean this Garvin fella's so stuck on Suzy that he bumps off her boyfriends?'

'Some lover, ain't he?' she commented.

'The man's crazy.'

'He certainly is. It's strange how love hits some folk, though. I guess we all go crazy in different ways when we're in love.'

'No dame would make me give a song and dance,' I said.

'No?' There was mockery in her tones. 'What's good for burns?' she added casually.

'Tannic acid jelly,' I said, not thinking what was in her mind.

She took a jar from the medicine cabinet, put her foot on the edge of the bath and pulled up her skirt. I remembered then why she would be wanting the ointment.

'Gee, I'm sorry about that,' I said.

'If it leaves a scar, I'll never forgive you.'

I began to feel a little hot under the collar. There was something kinda nice about the way she didn't seem to mind me being there while she dabbed on ointment and tightened her suspenders – kinda breathtaking, too.

I began to notice other things, too.

'Does it worry you?' she asked coolly. She knew I was looking at her and she was liking it.

'I guess I'm sorry I tore your dress, too.'

'I'd feel better in another blouse.'

She walked out from the bathroom across to the bedroom. I lounged after her and stood leaning against the doorpost while she changed. I didn't trust myself to get any closer.

'I'd like to think that you weren't standing there watching to prevent me from starting something,' she said. 'I'd like to think that you're standing there to peek at me.'

'But that's why I am standing ...' I began.

Her ripple of laughter interrupted me.

'Okay,' I grumbled, 'have fun with me.' I ground out the cigarette in an ashtray and refused to look at her. A few moments later she came over and took me by the arm.

'I'm sorry,' she said. ' I didn't mean to rib you, but you sounded so cocky about being in love that I just had to take you down a peg.'

'Okay,' I snarled. 'Button up your blouse and spill some more about Garvin.'

'Now you're offended.'

'Stow it, will ya. Just tell me where this Garvin fella hangs out.'

'Now, look,' she said determinedly. 'You're not going to get any big knight errant ideas about paying off Garvin, are you? He's a big noise around here. With luck you might only end up in a nice clean sack with a cut throat for asking questions. You're much too nice a guy to fool around in a sack that way.'

'Look. I may be a nice guy. But I had a friend, a sweet kid who right now is laid out on a cold white slab. Some folks might think nothing about it. But I'm not made that way.'

Her eyes were kinda sleepy and serious. 'It's got you on the raw. You're serious about this thing, aren't you?'

'So what?'

'Suzy's not gonna like it.'

'And why won't Suzy like it?'

'Because,' she said. 'Because Suzy's so madly in love with Garvin that she'd die for him.'

She poured out the drinks for a change.

'I don't get it,' I said. 'The Garvin fella gives Suzy hell and yet she'd die for him. It don't make sense.'

'Women never do make sense,' she replied. 'Not when they're in love.'

'Why don't Suzy get hitched with this fella?'

'Why?' She swung around on me. 'You ask me why. You, who've had your friend killed before your eyes. Would you hitch yourself to one of the dirtiest, low-down racketeers that ever lived? Would you marry a killer a hundred times over, a man whose hands are covered in blood, a man whose wealth has been made from the flesh and blood of others?'

'But she's in love with him, you say.'

'Can she help that? Hasn't she fought against it with every ounce of willpower her body's got?'

'It sounds screwy to me,' I told her.

'It is screwy. Life's like that.'

I sat down and fumbled for another cigarette. She

walked across to the phone and picked it up. I hardly noticed what she was doing until I heard her say:

'Suite 69. Will you serve dinner for two, please?'

First thing next morning I went to the bank and drew out my war gratuity. I'd put it away for a rainy day and it had come. I addressed an envelope to Lola's mother and sent the cash anonymously by registered post. It wasn't gonna replace Lola, but it'd help the old lady along for a while.

Then I went back to my hotel and fished out my service revolver. I wasn't supposed to have it, but somehow I'd got so used to having it around while I was winkling out Japs, that I felt I ought to keep it.

It was big and heavy, not the kinda gun you could stick in your jacket pocket. But it was well-cleaned and oiled and could blow a sizable hole in an elephant.

Then I got busy sewing the holster into my waistcoat, underneath the armpit. That was the best way to carry around a gun that size, I figured.

I did all this quite coolly and determinedly. I didn't think that I was going out to kill a man. It wasn't like that at all. I was just going out to some mopping-up. I felt like a rat-catcher must feel when he sets off to do his daily round.

I'd got Garvin's address from Joel – Joel being Blondie's sister. It was the Golden Peacock, like the taxi-jockey said. I'd got lots of other things from Joel, too, after we'd had dinner the previous night. I was getting to feel quite strong about that dame. She was tough, she was loyal and … well, I guess I was failing fast.

When I put on my jacket and looked in the mirror, the bulge of the gun couldn't be seen. That was what I wanted. But it was going to be a job getting it out from its holster. I just had to hope that I'd get an easy break.

There was an automatic café on the corner of my block. I went in, helped myself to ham and eggs and coffee and got that stowed under my belt and then set off.

I was surprised at my coolness. At times like this, just before an advance way back in the jungle, there'd always been that kinda suppressed excitement that kept every nerve on edge, waiting for something to break. But it wasn't like that now. I just knew that I was going out to kill or be killed, and it didn't seem to matter to me one way or the other.

Some folks might think I was doing a dopey kinda thing. The police are paid to take care of guys like Garvin. But I wanted to handle this job personally. Besides, from what I'd heard around town about Garvin, the cops wouldn't have much chance to take care of him the way I'd do it. That's what politics do.

I walked because it felt good to get exercise and I needed some fresh air too. It took me about an hour to get to Garvin's hangout. And a nice hangout it was too. Like the Ritz and Mindy's coiled into one.

Even though it was mid-afternoon, a show was on. I walked inside and a commissionaire bowed me to the check desk, where I left my hat in charge of a long-legged dame whose skirts were higher than the bottom of her pants. And it was a physical impossibility for the bottom of her pants to be any higher at that.

I tossed her a dime and was ushered to a table by an effusive head waiter who almost scraped his forehead on the ground. Two snaps of his fingers and a waiter appeared miraculously and handed me a menu.

I hardly looked at it. 'Bring me a Rye.'

Just then came a roll on the drums, the lights went out all over the place and a single flashlight stabbed through the blackness outlining one of the slickest lookers I'd ever seen.

She had a rich, deep voice, just right for the slow blues she crooned. It was a rich, voluptuous voice that had some magical quality of softness and comfort. The customers liked it. They probably liked her too. From where I was, I could see a lot of her. The backless evening dress she wore had only the most slender of straps to hold it in position, and whenever she moved, the front of her dress opened tantalisingly. The skirt was split too, from ankle to waist, and there didn't seem to be anything under the dress. And the dame did a lot of moving too, rippling her arms and swaying her waist. I wasn't surprised the customers applauded until they got an encore.

From way over on my right I caught a wisp of voices.

'That Garvin dame is good!'

'Good for what?' followed by a snigger.

Then the band began to play the 'St Louis Blues'.

The waiter brought my Rye.

'Her name Garvin?' I asked, thumbing towards the spotlight.

'Yes, sir. I thought everybody knew that.'

'Any relation to Nat Garvin?'

'His sister, sir.'

'Will she have a drink with me?'

'Only by appointment, sir. Have you an appointment?'

'Well, not exactly. But if you'd give her this ...'

I took a card from my pocket and scribbled on it hurriedly.

'Got an envelope?'

'I'll get one, sir.'

When he came back, I'd finished writing. I slipped the card in the envelope, sealed it carefully and gave it to him with a five-dollar bill.

Then it was just a question of waiting.

The act finished. She took a dozen bows and retired behind the curtain. The band struck up and couples drifted onto the floor and danced under softened lights.

She approached from behind so that I didn't know she was there until she'd had time to look me over.

'Mr Janson?' she said.

I stood up. 'I hope you'll excuse me ...' I began.

She jerked her head at the waiter who was standing there, and sat down. As soon as the waiter was gone, she leaned forward across the table.

'What's this about my life being in danger?'

' I hope you're gonna take this easy,' I said. 'I'm not just a rubberneck wanting to guzzle Scotch with you and try dating you up for the evening. That message was a phoney. But I've still gotta talk with you.'

She looked at me calculatingly.

'Start talking. And it'd better be good.'

'I'm new in this town,' I said. 'I've just got outa the services. A fella I used to know told me that if I ever wanted a job, Nat Garvin would be the fella to see.'

'So what?'

'He's a difficult man to see, I've been told.'

'And ...?'

'Aw gee, lady. Give me a break, willya? I thought you'd be a sport and give me an introduction.'

She sat back and looked at me hard. 'You've got a nerve,' she said. She was wearing a cape around her shoulders, and as she leaned back her arms were revealed. Beneath the powder she'd used to set off the spotlight I caught sight of a vicious bruise just above the elbow.

'I'm not asking much,' I wheedled. 'I only want a chance to talk to the boss.'

'Why don't you apply to the head waiter?'

I didn't reply at once. Instead I made a great play, pulling out my cigarette-case, offering it to her and lighting up.

I blew out a long plume of smoke and said:

'That's not the kinda graft I'm after. I'd like something a little more risky and a lot more profitable.'

'And who was the fella who told you to come here?'

'Tiny Farrant,' I replied promptly.

'And who's he?'

'He's a Chicago operator,' I told her. 'He moved in on the Spencer territory after prohibition.'

She sat there looking at me so long I began to think she'd gone to sleep with her eyes open.

'All right,' she said at last. 'You'd better come with me.'

She stood up and I stood up, too. With my elbow I nudged my side and felt the comforting bulge of the revolver. So far so good. If my luck held, in a few minutes I'd be blasting hell outa Nat Garvin. For the first time, it struck me that I might get the chair for this, if the clean-up didn't show that Garvin was behind the Florida stick-up. Otherwise I might get out in a coupla years with good conduct.

She led the way and I followed. We went around the walls, around to a door marked 'Office.'

She had to knock before it opened, and right the

other side was a thug with a hare-lip. He looked at me enquiringly.

'We're going up to see Nat,' she told him.

He nodded and stood aside. The dame led me over to a private lift. I opened the gates and stood aside to let her in. Then as I stepped into the lift a bell rang.

The girl gave me a queer look. 'You rodded up?' she asked.

I caught on then to the bell. 'Why, no,' I told her.

'Okay.' .

She pressed a button and we sped up. When the lift stopped, the doors opened automatically, and as I stepped out, a coupla fellows lined up aside me. Both of them deftly ran their fingers over me, and at once they located my gun. Even before I realised it, a hand was lugging my revolver from its holster, and as I realised that all my chances of settling Garvin's hash were about to disappear, I decided to fight for it. .

I swung suddenly and clopped the fella on my left under the chin. He went flying backwards, and as I turned to grapple with the man on my right, my head exploded, darkness swam up and around me and I plunged down and down, twisting and twirling.

It was the pain across my forehead that made me not want to open my eyes. Somewhere voices were talking and I knew I had to move. But I couldn't move. My muscles weren't working and my head was one mass of pain.

A cold sluice of water dashed against my face. Somewhere, somebody groaned, and vaguely I knew it came from me. Again the water dashed against my face and trickled down my collar. I opened my eyes and raised a hand to the back of my head. Something warm and sticky got on my fingers,

Another sluice of water enabled me to swim up into consciousness.

I was sitting in a deep armchair. On either side of me were the men who'd met me as I stepped out of the lift. One of them was holding an empty glass in one hand and a decanter in the other. From the look in his eyes, I guessed he'd liked to have slung the glass at me as well. Instinctively I knew he was the guy I'd slugged, and the swelling on his jaw seemed to bear me out.

I looked hazily around me. Garvin's sister was leaning against the mantelpiece, with a cigarette drooping from her mouth. Opposite me was a huge, streamlined desk made from black glass, with chromium fittings. Behind it sat one of the most handsome men I'd ever set eyes on.

When I say handsome, I mean he's the kinda guy I think women would find handsome. He had dark, wavy hair, exquisitely formed features and the air of a lord.

He was the last kind of person I'd have thought Nat Garvin to be.

The expression on his face was of benign consideration.

'I trust, Mr Janson, that you'll excuse my friend's rather crude method of reviving you.'

It was a deep chair and I had to reach out and grab the arms to pull myself up. Simultaneously, two hands grabbed me by the shoulders and thrust me back roughly.

'You'll be more comfortable, sitting,' said Garvin.

He picked up a gold letter-opener and began to pry at his fingernails.

'My sister informs me you wished to see me.'

I thought quickly. I hadn't got within an ace of doing what I wanted. I had to wriggle out of this jam some way to get another chance later on.

'I wanted a job,' I said thickly.

'Do you always ask for a job with a gun under your armpit?'

'Force of habit,' I said.

'Dangerous things to carry. They get you into trouble. But of course, you've found that out already. And ... er, your letters of introduction?'

'I ain't got any.'

Garvin blew gently on his nails and then polished them carefully on the sleeve of his jacket.

'This friend of yours who gave you my name ... Mr ... er ...?'

'Tiny Farrant,' I said quickly.

'I don't know the gentleman.'

'He knew you all right.'

Garvin laid down his paper-knife and looked me straight in the eyes. When he spoke, his voice took on a keen edge.

' Listen, Janson. I can use men who can look after themselves. But they have to have references. I don't know the man you've talked about. But if you're made of the kinda stuff I want, you'll get references. And you'll get them from people I know. When you've got them, come and see me again. And next time, ask for me at the door. And don't come rodded up.'

I nodded, which made my head hurt more. I touched my scalp tenderly and winced. The girl came over from the mantelpiece and looked at my head.

'Hold still a minute.'

I held still while she dabbed with her handkerchief. Then she tipped some Rye from a decanter at the sideboard onto her handkerchief and dabbed again.

After a while she said, 'Well, that's cleaned up a bit.'

'Thanks, lady,' I said.

She pulled a face when she looked at the bloody mess her handkerchief had become, and dropped it in a wastepaper basket. 'That's the last time I try the good Samaritan act,' she said.

'Oh yes,' said Nat suddenly. He got up from the desk. He was a tall, slim man, but the width of his shoulders showed he possessed excellent physique. 'Yes, Gwen, my dear, you brought Mr Janson up here, didn't you.'

Somehow his voice had undertaken a change. There was a menace in it that couldn't be pinned down.

He came from around his desk and stood in front of her so that the top of her bead came level with his chin. She stood there with her hands at her sides as though she was petrified.

'You brought Mr Janson up here without receiving instructions.'

She broke in on him quickly. 'But I knew it was all right, Nat. There's always two of your boys ...'

Completely unexpectedly he suddenly brought back his hand and slapped her hard across the face so that she pitched halfway across the room, tripped on a pouffe and sprawled on the floor.

The expression on his face didn't alter. He looked down at her with a good-humoured expression as she first got on all fours and then began to stand up. He suddenly brought his fist down on her head with such force that she smacked flat on her face again.

'Take it easy, Nat,' said one of the men. 'She's got a show tonight. Don't mark her.'

Gwen gave a sob. But she had enough savvy to

stay put where she was. Nat waited, and when she didn't get up, he prodded her with his toe.

'Do you know better?' he asked.

'Yes, Nat,' she said. 'I won't do it again, ever.'

'Get up,' he said.

She edged away from him apprehensively and slowly got to her feet, expecting every minute to be knocked down again. There was a deep crimson stain on her cheek where his hand had caught her.

'Now take Mr Janson downstairs again,' he said.

'Yes, Nat,' she said, scared. 'I'll take him down.'

She pulled up her shoulder strap, which had come awry, and one of the men gave her her wrap. I got up slowly, feeling as mad as hell and as weak as a kitten. I wanted to trample Garvin's face with hobnail boots, but I'd have been crazy to start anything.

'I hope to be seeing you soon, Mr Janson,' said Garvin.

' I'll be back,' I promised. 'I'll get all you want and I'll be around again.'

'I hope next time we shall meet under happier conditions,' he said. I could have slugged him on the jaw right then just for his oily, cocky manner.

Gwen walked in front along the corridor. I followed, and Garvin's two hoods walked one each side of me. When we got to the lift, Gwen stepped in and I followed. Just as the gates were about to close, I suddenly remembered.

'Hey, what about my gun?'

'Don't worry, buddy. You'll get that next time you call, perhaps.'

There was no point in arguing. The lift gates closed and down we went.

I looked at Gwen.

'I'm real sorry I caused all that fuss,' I said.

Without thinking, she raised a hand to her cheek.

'That's all right,' she said. 'Nat loses his temper sometimes. But he's always been like that since he was a kid.'

'He didn't oughta treat you that way.'

She looked at me curiously. 'What's the matter, bright-eyes, feel sorry for me?'

'I don't like to see dames treated that way.'

She laughed, a deep, rich laugh.

'It was my own fault. I knew Nat wouldn't like it.'

'Why'dya do it, then?'

'Ask me again, fella. Perhaps I thought you'd like a break.'

'I'd like to make it up to you some way.'

'Okay, you can.'

'Yeah?'

'Take me home. My next show is tonight. I could do with a sleep.'

She'd closed the lift gates and we began to walk towards the door opening onto the restaurant. All the time, I'd been memorising every inch of the way so I'd know my way again.

'I ain't got my car with me.'

'Use mine,' she said.

But instead of going through into the restaurant we went out another way into a courtyard. There was a big, streamlined cream and green car drawn up outside. Gwen got behind the steering wheel and I sidled into the seat beside her. As she started up the engine, a man came out from a small office and opened wide the courtyard gates. Gwen let in the gear and we swung out into the traffic.

8

'Come up and have a drink,' she said.

'Didn't you want to have a sleep?'

'What's the matter? Scared of me?'

' I could do with a drink. Can do most times.'

'I've got the best,' she said.

As soon as we got inside, she took off her wrap, threw it across the back of a settee and went across to the sideboard and poured out a couple of drinks.

'Here's to Nat,' she said.

I looked at her, but she meant it, so I drank it down and handed back the glass for another. Seeing her under a spotlight at a distance in that dress and seeing her close up were two different things. I began to feel uncomfortable – a pleasant uncomfortableness.

'These shoes are killing me,' she said, and took them off.

That meant bending up her knee, and her leg came right out through the split skirt. There was another bruise high up on her thigh.

'Did Nat do that?'

'What? Oh, that. Yeah, I guess so.'

'Why do you stand for it? He's got no call to knock

you about that way.'

'Nat don't mean it,' she said. 'He's a good fella, only his temper gets the better of him.'

I had another drink quick. I guess I just didn't see it the way she did.

'You know something?' she said.

I looked at her. There was something about her that was getting me.

'I took a fancy to you.'

'Yeah.'

'When I first met you there was something I liked about you. That's why I took you up to Nat's office. I knew he'd be mad about it.'

She'd come close to me and was standing there, kind a waiting for something. I didn't need to be told what it was. I reached out and grabbed her by the shoulders and kissed her. She put her arms around me and strained tight against me. My fingers explored the warm, smooth softness of her flesh. Every curve she had was moulding into my body, and then she bit my lip. She bit so hard I couldn't stand it. I got her head between my hands and hammered hard. But she clung to me, and her teeth gouged even deeper into my lip so that my mouth filled with blood. The pain drove me into a frenzy. I pummelled and tore at her with my hands and at last she let go. I sent her flying across the room, sprawling into the settee, where she lay, smiling at me with a sleepy kinda look in her eyes.

There was a thin dribble of blood running from her deep red lips to her chin, and she must have known that in my frenzy I'd broken her shoulder-straps. The top of her dress wasn't where it should've been; it was in her lap.

'You bitch,' I said, wiping my mouth with my

handkerchief. I was panting hard.

'Did I hurt you?' she asked slyly.

'Why d'you do it?'

She got up and came over to me. I couldn't help myself. I took her in my arms again. She didn't bite no more, and after that there wasn't any holding back.

I got back to my apartment about dusk, and the first thing I did was to get under the shower and pelt my skin alternately with boiling water and then with ice-cold water. There's nothing like that for freshening up. Especially when you've been slugged, bitten and made love to, all in one afternoon.

I hopped outa the bath and dried myself briskly and weighed up the situation so far.

I'd taken on myself the responsibility of cleaning out that rat, Garvin. I had as much chance of getting on shooting terms with him on his own premises as I had of getting into the UNO conference – thanks to his bodyguard.

Therefore I had to get Garvin when he was out in the open. But that wasn't gonna be so easy. I'd have to hang around his joint with a gat in my pocket perhaps for hours, and then I'd only get a chance to sling lead as his car swung out from the courtyard. And the betting was that his car had bullet-proof glass.

The odds should have been on my side. Most fellas who plug other fellas usually wanna scram before the law puts the arm on them. But once I'd got Garvin, I didn't care much what happened to me. Those years in the jungle made me value life pretty low, and after all, this was just a different sort of jungle with a different kind of Jap to sling lead at.

But even so, it was gonna be difficult.

If there was only some way of locating Garvin when he'd left his fortress!

Something Joel said about Blondie came into my mind. Garvin was in love with Blondie and bumped off any fella that gave her a whirl.

If Garvin was that crazy about her, he'd be trying to locate her right now. And Garvin had ways of finding out things he wanted to know.

So if I could find Blondie, park on her doorstep and wait for Garvin to arrive, I might meet him on more even terms.

But that only put me back where I started. Because I didn't know where Blondie was, and all that Joel could tell me was that Blondie had taken a powder and was gonna stop outa town until Garvin folded up.

I finished drying myself and went out to get my clothes.

There was a tough looking fella lounging back in my favourite chair with his heels on the table and one of my best cigars stuck in the corner of his mouth.

'Hiyah, Adam,' he said pleasantly.

I eyed him steadily and reached for a dressing gown.

'Who the hell are you? Satan?'

He flicked ash on my carpet, took another cigar, inspected it carefully and stowed it away in his waistcoat pocket.

I picked tip a heavy bronze ash-tray and dropped it on his foot. He howled and clutched his foot with both hands. It was a difficult feat for him on account of his waistline.

'My God, I'll get you for that,' he threatened.

'Who let you in?'

He winced and tenderly caressed his boot. 'I'm asking the questions,' he said.

'Yeah.' I walked over to the phone and picked it up, watching him warily meantime.

'Police,' I said into the mouthpiece.

He fumbled in his pocket and flashed a card at me. I put down the phone again.

'Whadya want, copper?' I said.

'Branger is the name,' he said, slowly. 'And I want a number of things. In the first place I want some straight answers, and in the second place I want your guts for garters on account of my toe.' He gingerly put his foot back on the carpet and stood up.

He was a big man, almost as broad as he was tall.

'I'm gonna poke you on the snout for that,' he said.

I didn't doubt he was gonna try. I kept my distance.

'What's the racket?' I demanded. 'What did ya come busting in here for?'

He fitted his thumbs in his armpits and rocked on heels and toes.

'Some fellas take a warning, others don't,' he said. 'Are you a bright guy?'

' I've still got my head on my shoulders.'

'Yeah.' He rocked backwards and forwards some more and eyed me carefully.

' Just outa the Army, arncher?'

'Yeah. And I still managed to keep my head on my shoulders.'

'Not in the mood for a reglar job, I guess.'

'Whatya getting at?' I demanded. 'I'm a reglar citizen, see. I pay my rates and taxes. I keep on the right side of John Law and haven't even had a ticket for speeding. If there's anything on your mind, spill it.'

'Civvy life's different from the Army, fella. Ya don't go around shooting up folk in civil life.'

I chilled all over as I remembered Garvin had kept my gun. I picked up a cigarette and lit it, playing for time and hoping my hand wasn't gonna shake. It didn't. But the copper watched me all the time, steady like.

'And …?' I said.

'And,' he repeated. 'And any young fella that thinks he can outbid the law is on a bad bet.'

I blew smoke down my nostrils and said, 'Go sing psalms in another alley.'

I never knew anyone could move so quick. He looked all size and belly. But one moment he was standing there looking at me and the next moment he had one hand around my throat and the other twisting my arm behind my back.

'Listen, runt,' he said, and his ugly puss was pressed up close to mine. 'Don't get any smart ideas about easy living. I'm warning ya now, see, while you've still gotta chance to pull up. We've got the finger on ya. Garvin can give ya protection, sure. He's got all the mouthpieces in town lined up to sing sweet on his side of the fence. But he can't beat the rap all the time. And when Garvin goes down, he'll go down good and long with probably a burning at the end of it. Likewise anyone who's daffy enough to pull on his oar.'

He flung me halfway across the room. I brought down a small table and a lamp with me.

'I'm warning you, smartie,' he said. 'Stay clear from Garvin. If you've got the guts to do a man's job, ya can get an enrolment form at headquarters, if it's excitement ya want.'

I got up unsteadily. I wanted to take a poke at his big puss for slinging me around that way, but it's no dice hitting dicks. They yell copper on ya, and get you stuck in the pen on a charge of assault and battery. I just swallowed and said nothing.

'Just don't let 'em get another report at headquarters that you're calling on Garvin,' he warned.

'Say,' I gasped. 'Y'mean you case that joint so close ya know who Garvin sees?'

He ignored me, turned his back and walked over to the door. He paused with his hand on the doorknob.

'I'm gonna save it up for ya, Janson. Some time, I'm gonna remember to repay that bouncing ash-tray.'

He shut the door behind him so softly I didn't even hear the latch click.

That brief little interview showed me just where the cops stood in relation to Garvin. There they were, all lined up to take action against him, but they just couldn't put the finger on him. All they could do was throw a scare into small fry who teamed up with him.

Once again it all came back to being my responsibility.

Yeah, it was my affair. I was gonna bump Garvin and I was gonna take the rap for it.

But how?

I hadn't even got a gun now.

I finished dressing and went down to Mike's Beannery.

''Lo, Hank.'

'Hiya, Mike.'

He dished up a steak and eggs. I sat at the counter, eating. There were three or four other fellas along the counter, but nobody right close.

I caught Mike's eye. He came over and wiped down the counter.

'How d'ya kill rats?' I asked.

'That's a professional job,' he said.

'Yeah?'

'Sure is. Ya get in touch with a company and they send a coupla fellas with the whole outfit; poison gas and everything.'

'Ya got me wrong, Mike. I mean rats.'

'That's what I thought you said.'

'But some rats are different.'

'Sure thing. Some are black, some are brown, some are fat, some ...'

'I know. I know.'

He gave me a strange look. 'What'ya getting at, Hank?'

'Human rats,' I told him.

His face didn't move a muscle, but he went on cleaning the counter further down the bar. He was thinking it over.

He brought over a sweet, took away my dirty plate and came back with a fork and spoon.

'Don't be a screwy kid,' he advised.

'This ain't screwy, Mike. It's plain commonsense.'

'Folks are a long time dead, Hank. They say the chair sometimes takes half an hour to burn you dead.'

'I used to know a kid named Lola,' I said.

'Yeah. I used to know Lola. Nice kid.'

'Too nice to finish that way.'

'Yeah.'

There was a long pause .

'You sure you know what you're doing?'

'I know what I'm doing, Mike. I'm gonna shoot a rat. But it's tough to do it without a gat.'

'You know I've got a licence for mine. It can be traced.'

'I'll take care of that, Mike. There won't be no trouble.'

He was still uncertain, worried.

'I don't like ya doing this, Hank.'

'I'm gonna do it, Mike. I'm gonna do it. You can make it easy.'

He shook his head and worried over a coupla dishes he served further along the counter. He didn't come near me after that. I sat there and smoked two cigarettes and kept watching him. At last he came over to me.

'You set on this thing, Hank?' He was genuinely unhappy.

'I mean it, Mike,' I said quietly.

He leaned across the counter. 'I keep it in the dresser drawer in the office. If you go out the back way on account of going to the toilet, you'll pass the dresser.'

Somebody called for a roll. Mike left me, and a few seconds later I got up and casually strolled through the office.

When I came back, I finished my coffee. Mike wouldn't look at me. I got up, left a dime by the plate and went out. Mike didn't even glance up at me.

I knew he was smart enough to ring the cops pretty soon and advise them his gun had been knocked off. That would leave him in the clear for anything that happened afterwards. I went home to get a good night's sleep. I reckon I needed it.

9

It was hot the next afternoon. I parked my Chevrolet and got the desk clerk to call Joel. She musta been waiting on me because she came down at once.

'I'm glad you wanna come,' I told her, taking her in with my eyes. She was a quiet dresser but a nifty dresser just the same. She knew how to wear clothes.

'Do I look good?' she asked.

'You look good to me. Got your swimsuit?'

'Naturally, since we're going swimming.'

'I'll bet you'll look good in that, too.'

'Is that why you suggested swimming?'

We were walking over to my car by this time. The sun was beating down on the hard tarmac and bouncing back and hitting us in the face.

'Still got doubts about me, eh?'

'I never trust a man, not unless he's got his hands and feet tied.' She laughed, making a joke outa what could have been a gentle warning.

We drove out through town, talking all the while about this and that. She had a nice line in gab, free and easy, none of the carefully thought-out phrases that some dames learn off by heart and repeat all over again because they don't know anything else to say. Every now and again I glanced down at her knees. A car's the best thing for showing a dame's knees.

'Where we heading?'

'I know a place,' I told her. 'Not many folk get around to it. There's sand dunes and no rocks to knock yourself against.'

'Tell me why you really rang me up and asked me to come,' she said.

'Do I have to have a reason other than the obvious?'

'Okay. You like the way I look, walk and talk. But what's the other reason?'

'You're too modest,' I told her. 'Can't a fella wanna be with you just for the sake of being with you?'

'I should hope I'm not too hard to look at.'

' Well, cutey, I'm finding I kinda like to have you around.'

'You wouldn't want to be pumping me about Suzy and where she is?'

I gave her a sidelong glance. She was looking straight at me with her wide eyes.

'I thought you might let up on some dope about Blondie,' I confessed. 'But ... I'm sure gonna enjoy being with you.'

' Let's get this straight, Hank. I'd like to enjoy this afternoon. I guess I like being with you, too. But I don't know where Suzy is. Now you can turn right around and take me back or carry on. But if you carry on, don't spoil the day by asking about Suzy. There's nothing I can tell you.'

'On the level?'

'On the level,' she said.

That was tough. But even if she didn't know where

Blondie was, I wasn't gonna pass up an afternoon with Joel.

'I'll forget all about Blondie,' I told her.

I knew a way down to the beach where I could take the car. Keeping on the beach where it was gravel meant the wheels didn't sink. I threaded in around the back of some sand dunes. It was deserted around there and we were set for a twosome.

I lugged a hamper out from the back or the car and a coupla bottles of beer. The sun was pouring down and my shirt was sticking to me.

'Whadya wanna do, swim first?' I asked.

'Swim first,' she said decidedly. 'We can lie in the sun afterwards and make pigs of ourselves while we get brown.'

She got her costume and slid around the other side of a sand dune.

I slipped off my shoes and pushed my socks into them.

I took off my jacket, folded it and put it on a rock, I slipped off my shirt and trousers and was standing there in my underpants when I got a vicious jab in the ribs with a gun-barrel.

'Get your dukes well up and keep 'em there!'

It was such a surprise that I half-turned, without thinking. I turned right around into a knee that drove into the pit of my stomach. After that I lay on the sand and gasped for breath while my guts heeled over and over.

'Just lay there that way, dope, if you wanna keep healthy.'

I looked up at him through eyes spurting tears. I hadn't seen him before, but I wasn't gonna forget him in a hurry.

He was slim and sleek with a fedora on the back of his head. He had slit eyes, high cheekbones and a thin slit of a mouth. He was chewing a matchstick and holding his gun like a fella that's held guns before.

'Guess you'll know me, next time,' he said.

I didn't say anything. I was hoping that Joel would keep the other side of that sand dune and keep outa trouble.

'What's your name, sucker?'

I didn't answer and he moved in and drew back his pointed shoe.

'Janson,' I said quickly. I didn't want more trouble than necessary.

'Janson, eh?' It obviously didn't mean anything to him.

'What goes on?' I asked.

He chewed a match. I thought he wasn't gonna reply, but then:

'You'll be all right, buddy. Just keep your trap shut and you'll stop healthy.'

I was hoping like hell that Joel was gonna stay put. I thought she'd perhaps hear us talking or something and be warned. But then I heard her scream.

I half-rose and the foot swung in readiness again. His eyes didn't leave me for a moment and I hadn't a chance. I relaxed.

They'd got Joel, too. She'd got down to her briefs and bra when the fella got her, and she wasn't coming quietly. The fella bringing her had doubled her arms up behind her back and was marching her along in front of him.

'What kept ya so long, Froggy?' asked my man.

Froggy, a big-built fella with the face and arms of an ape, leered.

'The dame was giving a striptease act, Joe. Too bad she saw me before she got around to the seventh veil.'

'Too bad you don't keep your mind on the business.'

Joel gave a sudden squirming twist and kicked out. She didn't catch anybody, but Ape-arms gave her arms a severe wrench and the strap on her bra snapped.

I didn't stand a dog's, but I just had to do something.

I'd got to my knees by the time Joe's foot caught me. I was expecting it and tried to tuck my chin into my shoulder. It was like getting a kick from a mule. I took the full force of it partly on my chin and partly on my shoulder. It lifted me a coupla yards along the ground. As his foot swung a second time, I grabbed wildly. The shoe caught me on the chest, but I had him by the ankle. I yanked and Joe fell on top of me. His gun swung down and I jerked my head to one side. The barrel ripped down the side of my cheek and numbed my shoulder right down to my fingertips. I caught a glimpse of Joel struggling madly in the grip of Froggie, who had his big ape arms around her, his thick fingers gouging into her soft flesh.

Then the gun slashed down on my head and everything went into a red haze through which the intense stabbing pain in my head drove right through to my spine. I felt I was trying to move in a thick, sticky red substance. Then another sharp pain cleaved through the red stuff so that it slipped away from me, leaving me in nothingness.

There was a sack of coal pressing down on my head, thrusting my face into the ground so that I couldn't breathe. I fought madly for breath, willing my lungs to suck in air. The air ran into my lungs and I coughed and choked and nearly died with the effort of getting my breath, realising dimly that I'd sucked up water instead of air. The ground was moving beneath me, slipping, sliding, and then the next wave came and swirled around me, lifting me off the sand and floating me bumpingly along the beach.

I was tired, dreadfully tired. I hadn't the strength to move.

It was easier to lie and let the water rock me gently.

Another wave rolled me over, my head went under water and instinctively I clawed at the sand. My head was heavy with pain as though red hot rivets had been hammered into it.

I made the effort and crawled onto my knees. Another wave knocked me flat again. I shut my eyes tightly and crawled further up the beach, then I lay there and panted. I became conscious that the sun was going down, a wind was blowing up and I was feeling cold.

Painfully I turned over and sat up. I touched my head gingerly to make sure it was still all there. I had two lumps the size of ducks' eggs standing out on my scalp. I was beginning to be amazed that my head could take such punishment. I'd been slugged flat two days in succession.

After a while it grew upon me that Joel wasn't there. Those two hoodlums had either taken her off or salted her away with a rock around her ankles. That got me good and anxious. I got on my pins, rather weakly, and hunted around. My Chevrolet had gone. I found one of my shoes floating around on the surf. Joel's clothes were where she'd left them, and her bra was trampled into the churned-up sand. She'd put up a good fight.

I couldn't find the rest of my clothes. I guessed the tide had caught them up.

And that left me in a spot. Ten miles out of town, no transport, one shoe and my underpants. Not the best of travelling equipment.

But get back to town I must, because there was only one answer to finding out what had happened to Joel, and that was to find out from Garvin. I must've been a dope not to see it before. Garvin wanted Blondie, I wanted Blondie. I'd tackled Blondie's sister to find out what she knew. And that was just what Garvin was doing.

And if anything had happened to Joel …

I stumbled up the beach and made the highway. The first car that came along was driven by two old dames. They slowed down and then suddenly accelerated. I can't say I blame them. I must've looked a queer proposition.

I had to wait 20 minutes before the next car came. I stepped out in the road and thumbed madly. The car pulled up and the driver looked out.

'What's the racket?'

'I've been robbed and slugged.' I said. 'Get me into town, willya?'

He looked me over carefully.

'Hold on, buddy,' he said. 'I'll be back.'

He got into gear and away so smartly he nearly took my toes with him. I cursed and sat down and waited. I was really cold by this time. My body was blue and my teeth were chattering.

Ten minutes passed and then a car approached from town.

I just sat there, but the car pulled up with a squeal of brakes, slewed around and I caught sight of uniforms.

The cop got out and tossed me a rug.

'Hop in, fella. I don't know if you're a nut or if you've been slugged like you told the other fella, but you can't go to town either way wearing that fig-leaf.'

I climbed into the back seat.

'Got a slug?' I asked through chattering teeth.

One of them produced a flask from his hip pocket. I took a deep gulp.

'Take it easy, fella,' he said. 'We're gonna want you to answer questions.'

I lowered my head so he could see the two lumps. He gave a long, low whistle.

'That should take care of a lot of the questions,' I told him.

It was two hours before I got outa the can. Two solid hours of questioning.

'What did the fella look like?'

'What did he have on you?'

'What were you doing on the beach?'

'Come across fella, what did be look like?'

Two hours it took me to convince those cops that I'd been robbed and slugged. If there'd been any trimmings to my story I'd never have got loose in under 24 hours.

So I kept my story short and neat. I said I'd gone swimming, began to undress, got slugged by somebody I didn't see and woke up with my car and money missing.

That way I got outa the cop-shop in what was, to them, short time. A squad-car took me back to my apartments and escorted me upstairs. I guess I caused a bit of a sensation coming home that way and walking up the steps with a blanket around me looking like Chief Sitting Bull.

I gave the cops a quick drink, got them off the

premises and then began to dress like mad.

Ever since I'd recovered consciousness on the beach, one thought had been in my mind – Joel. Throughout the third-degree and the journey home I'd been half-insane with worry about her. I knew the cops would be no good. They wouldn't bust into Garvin's joint just on my say-so. This was a job I'd have to handle myself.

My eye fell on the clock and gave me an idea. I picked up the telephone and dialled. My heart jumped when Gwen Garvin crooned her low 'Hello' into my ear.

'Are you just off to the show, honey?'

'You've just caught me in time.'

'Say, sugar, mind if I come along to hold your hand?'

'I'd like it swell, but you'll have to hurry.'

'Meet you at the car park in five minutes,' I promised.

I slammed down the receiver, fished around in the bottom of my wardrobe and uncached Mike's revolver. I stowed it away in my hip pocket. I was self-conscious about the lumps in my nut, and I pulled out an old grey fedora that I hadn't worn in years. It wasn't a bad fit and it hid my eruptions.

I was as good as my word. I made Gwen's place in four minutes 45 seconds, using about a week's wear of tyres and brakes in the short distance. I parked beside Gwen's big, streamlined green and cream limousine.

She arrived almost at the same time, and I could see beneath her wrap that she was already dressed for the show.

The meeting was a little hot and a little passionate, but she said there wasn't much time before the curtain call, so we both climbed into her car and we started off.

There was a kinda dreamy, satisfied look in Gwen's eyes.

'Whatya been doing today, honey?' I asked.

'Nothing, much,' she said airily.

'Been sleeping this afternoon?'

She smiled as if remembering something deliciously pleasing.

'I just hung around with Nat for a while, then went home to get a change of costume.'

'That all?' I was a little anxious and jerked the question at her. She looked at me quickly.

'Checking up on me?'

'Nope,' I said quietly. 'Just wondered what you were doing.'

While I was talking I was planning in my mind. This way I'd get into Garvin's place. After that everything was up to my knowledge of the place and Mike's gun.

When we rolled around to the courtyard, Gwen honked a coupla times, the courtyard gates swung open and we rolled through quietly. The gates closed behind us.

She looked at her watch.

'I'll have to hurry.'

'You're not on for 20 minutes, yet,' I said.

'Got to get my warpaint on.'

I stuck close to Gwen as we went in the back way. The thug with the hare-lip was waiting there. He raised his eyebrows when he saw me.

'He's my buddy,' she said. 'He's okay.'

'Yeah,' I told Hare-lip. 'You and me will get along in this outfit, I hope.'

He didn't express a similar hope. He just stared at me with expressionless eyes.

We went through the door marked 'Private' into the restaurant. Gwen's dressing room was over on the other side.

'Sit down and have a Martini ready for me, sugar,' she ordered.

'Don't be away too long, honey.'

I sat down and gave an order to the waiter. Gwen disappeared the other side. I got up swiftly and walked over to the door I'd just come through and knocked on it. The second time I knuckled on it the door swung open about two inches and I was gazing into Hare-lip's eyes again.

'Miss Garvin's left her handbag in the car,' I said.

He opened the door and I kinda talked my way through it.

'She's got a letter in there for Nat and she wants to give it to him right away.'

By this time the door had shut behind me.

The dull, flat eyes watched me, and I couldn't tell whether he believed me or not.

'I'll just buzz out and get it,' I said, drifting towards the door to the courtyard. Then I stopped suddenly.

'Oh, yeah, Miss Garvin said I was to give you this and that you'd find it very helpful.'

I fished in my hip pocket and had the gun out and trained in a dead straight line on his navel before he knew what was happening. His flat eyes looked expressionlessly at the muzzle.

'Okay,' I breathed. 'One peep outa you and you're a dead duck. Now get moving up the passage.' I gestured with the gun.

Slowly and ponderously he turned around. I frisked him from behind and found a rod under his armpit. I slid it as a spare into my jacket.

'Get moving,' I said and jabbed the gun hard into his spine. I wasn't in a joking mood, with Joel in trouble.

When we got to the lift I made him open the doors. As I stepped in I heard the warning bell ring somewhere up above.

'Listen, punk,' I said, as we went up. 'I know there's a coupla of your pals waiting for us to step out, but if there's any blasting, you're gonna get it first, right in the base of the spine. And even if it doesn't kill you, you'll be interested to know it'll paralyse you for life.'

Hare-lip didn't speak. He hadn't said a word the whole time. Only by the taut way he strained his neck could I tell he knew well enough what I was talking about and that I meant it.

When the lift stopped, Hare-lip opened the gates. I had it all figured out. I was gonna shove Hare-lip to the left and blast the fella on the right. I hoped that Hare-lip and the other fella would be so tied up with each other that I'd get a chance to draw a bead on them.

But it wasn't necessary, because there was no reception party.

'Listen, Hare-lip,' I said, 'where are your two pals?' I jabbed hard with the gun.

He did his best. He kinda honked through his twisted mouth in a low bass, but what he said I just didn't get.

'Okay,' I interrupted him, 'just don't talk. I like you better that way.'

I knew where Garvin's office was. I poked Hare-lip along in front of me, along the corridor to the room at the end. I could hear voices inside.

I hadn't spent years in the army without learning the value of surprise.

Keeping my gun close up against Hare-lip's spine, I softly turned the door handle.

Then it was all timing.

With one thrust I crashed the door back on its hinges. My boot got well behind Hare-lip and propelled him into the centre of the room, where he sprawled out like a lizard lying in the sun. I stood framed in the doorway with my gun covering the whole room. But it was a different tableau from what I'd expected. I was after Garvin, among other things, and he wasn't there.

But what was there filled me with a cold fury that almost sent my finger pressing on the gun trigger again and again.

There was a heavy hat rack over on the wall. Suspended from it by her wrists, with her toes barely touching the ground, was Joel.

There hadn't been any additions made to her wardrobe since she'd been hijacked from the beach, and ugly, blood-streaked weals covered her back from neck to thigh. From the way her head was hanging, I knew she was out cold.

There were three other people in the room. Two of them were the thugs usually on guard at the lift. One of them was sprawled out in a chair, smoking a cigar, the second was holding a jug of water he was about to throw over Joel. The third person was Gwen.

It was just like a still of an action shot. The three of them kinda froze where they were, with their eyes turned to me.

I could see only one thing. That was the leather belt in Gwen's hand and the lustful, sadistic smile on her lips. It lasted only a moment, but it told me everything.

I couldn't keep the steel outa my voice.

'Get your mitts up and back up against that wall.

That's it, you too, Hare-lip. Now keep your hands up and turn around.'

I pulled Hare-tip's rod out of my pocket and moved up behind them. Hare-lip didn't even know it was happening. The gun kinda bounced off his skull. He slipped down quietly.

The second fella instinctively tried to dodge, but it didn't help him any. The third tried to protest.

'She made us do it ...' he began, and his hands moved to protect his head. I smacked his knuckles hard, and as he tore them away in agony I smacked him hard behind the ear.

'Say, honey,' drawled Gwen. 'I didn't know you could be so tough.'

There was complete confidence in her voice. She thought she had me running in circles, that I held a torch for her or something. It was as easy for her as it was for Hare-lip, because neither knew I was going to do it.

I stood looking down at them for a moment, fighting down a mad impulse to batter their heads until their brains oozed over the floor.

It was Joel moaning that really saved me from doing it.

I cut her down and fed her some whisky. She kept moaning and arching her back as though she was still being beaten. I fed her more whisky, bathed her temples and alternately slapped her cheeks and cushioned her head on my shoulder. Seeing her like that was tearing me up inside.

After a while, her eyes opened and she looked at me with recognition instead of that dull, pain-crazed look.

'Hank,' she whispered. 'You've come. I knew you'd come.'

10

It was quite a while before Joel was able to sit up and take notice properly. She was suffering terribly. Her back was one mass of flinching, quivering nerves. Every move she made sent pain chasing through her. When one of the plug-uglies showed signs of coming round, it was a pleasure to slap him cold again.

'Who did it?' I asked.

'She did it.' She pointed at Gwen, heaped limply against the wall. 'But she was only the instrument. Garvin wanted to know where Suzy was.'

'I know.' I could see if all happening, 'Garvin wanted information and Gwen liked getting it out of you.'

Joel gave a little gasp and bit her hand hard. She bit so hard the blood began to spurt from beneath her teeth. I got hold of her head and tried to pull her hand away. It was no good. I had to slap her real hard before she let go, and then she moaned and rocked backwards and forwards and tried to smash her head against the wall.

I got a firm grip on her. 'What'ya trying to do, kill yourself?'

'Suzy,' she moaned. 'He's gone to get Suzy. I told him where she is. I couldn't help it. I tried hard, but the pain was too much.'

'You said you didn't know,' I reminded her .

'That was so you wouldn't go looking for trouble. But he'll get Suzy now and he'll kill her.'

'You're crazy, kid. Why should he kill her?'

'Don't you see? She won't have him. He's gonna make sure nobody else has her. He'll kill her. He told me that's what he's gonna do.'

I thought quickly.

'Listen, Joel,' I said. 'You know where she is. We've gotta get to her first. I've got a little matter I want to clear up with Garvin myself.'

'He'll kill her,' she moaned.

I gripped her hard by one shoulder and ran my palm down her back. She shrieked with agony.

'Are you gonna stop getting hysterical?' I growled. 'Where's Blondie? We've got to get to her.'

'It's near Demurara, a little one-horse town. There's a shooting lodge there.'

I made a swift calculation. 'We can get there by daybreak, I figure, if we rip the skids off the car.'

'Garvin will get there first.'

'Maybe. But we won't be far behind.'

I looked at the four limp figures stretched out on the floor. 'We'll have to fix them so they don't cause trouble.'

There was a long curtain cord. I ripped it loose and jammed one end under the window sash. Keeping it taut, I made a loop in it about four feet along. I lugged Hare-lip out into the middle of the floor, fed his neck into the loop and pulled tight. Then further along the cord I made another loop and fixed a neck inside that. I did the same with the other fella, and that left me with a loose end. I tied that around a good, strong, heavy wardrobe. After that I doused the three of them with water until they came round. I didn't let them stand. I made them keep sitting, and when all three of them were sitting up and taking notice, I took in all the slack on the cord. Yeah, I guess it left them choking a bit, but after what had happened to Joel, I wasn't being squeamish. It was a nice tidy bit of work. The cord stretched across the room from window to wardrobe pretty near as tight as I could stretch it. Spaced at regular intervals along the cord were three heads. They sat there with their tongues hanging out and their fingers trying to ease the strain on their windpipes. It wasn't only that they couldn't move – they daren't! If one moved, he'd choke himself and his pals. It was a pretty set-up.

'Directly we get outa here, you take it on the lam to my apartments,' I told Joel. 'Leave everything to me. If it's possible to save Blondie, I'll do it.'

'Not on your life, Hank. I'm going with you.'

'Don't be crazy, honey. A journey like that in your condition will kill you.'

She got hold of me and wrapped her arms around me. I wanted to hold her, too, but I knew it'd hurt like hell to as much as lay a finger on her. I just let her hold onto me while all the time my blood mounted higher and higher so that I almost forgot where I was.

'I gotta go with you, Hank. Don't you see? It's got to be this way. It's you an' me together, all the time. Promise you'll let me go with you.'

What could I do? The crazy little fool.

'Okay, sweetie, you come along,' I conceded. I reckoned I could dump her just before trouble started.

She pushed herself away from me and looked down at herself despairingly.

'Yeah,' I said. 'You're not gonna walk around the streets in that piece of two by four without a cop wanting to know the whys and wherefores, apart from the obstruction rubbernecks would cause.'

'I gotta have something to wear.'

I turned Gwen over on her back. She was still out cold and breathing lightly. I began to think I might have slugged her a bit too hard. She was only a dame.

She didn't weigh much either, I noticed, as I picked her up and carried her over to the divan. I tumbled her onto it. I took her shoes off and gave them to Joel. They were a little big, but good enough for the job. Gwen was wearing the dress she'd been wearing when I first saw her. It didn't take long to strip that off, and I was just beginning to take an interest in what I was doing when Joel shouldered me aside.

'All right, big-eyes,' she said. ' I'll attend to this.'

I stood back and watched. Joel bent up and looked at me meaningfully. I turned around.

'You can look now,' said Joel a little later. I did look, but by this time Joel had wrapped a small tablecloth around Gwen. It wasn't a big cloth and it didn't cover a lot of ground, but it covered enough.

Then I had a good look at Joel, and it made my hair curl.

If Gwen looked the goods in that dress, then Joel was Jane Russell, Jean Harlow and Clara Bow all rolled into one.

'I hope you'll always wear dresses like that,' I said.

'We'll get around to that later,' said Joel. 'Meanwhile, what are we gonna do with this dame?'

'I guess we can tie her up, too.' I looked around for another piece of cord.

'Wait a minute,' said Joel, and there was a hard note in her voice. 'I'd like to figure out something extra special for this dame.'

With a determined look in her eyes she bent down

and picked up the strap Gwen had been wielding.

'Hey,' I said. 'Just a minute. We've had enough of that.'

'Keep your pants on,' she said.

She threaded the strap around Gwen, rolling her over onto her belly and pinioning her arms. When she began to pull the strap tight, Gwen moaned softly, showing the first signs of recovering consciousness. Joel shoved her foot in the middle of Gwen's back to get leverage. The strap creaked and flesh puckered up around the edges as Joel strained to make the next hole. When she'd done it, she rolled Gwen over to her back again.

'You can get a job trussing chickens for Christmas,' I told her. I was wondering what came next. I wasn't gonna stand for any more whippings. Not now I'd cooled down.

Joel took the water jug and poured what was left over Gwen, who moaned some more. Her eyelids fluttered and she moved her head.

There was grim determination in Joel's eyes. She slapped Gwen's face unmercifully until she opened her eyes fully. When she saw Joel glaring down at her she flinched away as far as she was able.

'Handkerchief,' Joel rapped at me. I obligingly supplied a handkerchief.

'Get me a couple of ties.'

I stripped the ties off the fellas, watching Joel meantime to see what she was up to.

'Open your mouth,' she told Gwen, and when she didn't open it quick enough she nearly knocked her head off her shoulders. Gwen opened her mouth to scream and into it went my handkerchief, and it was strapped into place with Hare-lip's tie. The way Joel tugged on that tie nearly cut Gwen's face in two.

Then Joel ran her hand up Gwen's neck, gathering

that beautiful waving hair into one single tress in the end of which she rapidly tied a thick knot. Then, with a strength I didn't suspect she possessed, she lugged Gwen off the bed and pulled her across the room – by her hair, of course. I saw the tears spurt from Gwen's eyes and her face contort as she screamed against my handkerchief.

I began to see the idea when Joel knotted another tie around Gwen's hair, passed one end over the hook of the hat rack and began to pull.

She hoisted Gwen into just the position she'd been in herself, only with this difference. Gwen was suspended by her hair, and only the tips of her toes touched the floor. Every time her toe muscles gave out she literally hung by the roots of her hair.

'And if nobody finds her for ten days I shan't worry,' said Joel.

I helped her on with Gwen's fur wrap, and when I saw again the way her back muscles flinched away from the softness of the lining, I couldn't feel any sympathy for Gwen. She'd sure asked for all she was getting.

We turned the light out after us, locked the door from the outside and threw the key down the lift-shaft. When we stepped out of the lift at the bottom, I gave Joel my pocket handkerchief and she wrapped it around her hair so as not to give the show away too easily.

We stepped out into the courtyard and Joel got into the driving seat of the green and cream limousine as quickly as possible. She hooted like I told her, and the fella in the office came out, gave one look at the car and opened the gates.

We drove out past him so quickly be didn't get a chance to have a good look. All he saw was Gwen's wrap and Gwen's car and that was enough for him.

A few blocks along we changed over and Joel got in

the back where she could stretch out on her belly. After all she'd gone through, she wasn't wanting to have her back jolted against cushions.

Just before we left town I stopped at a herbalist shop and got some ointment. First chance I had, I massaged it gently into her skin. She almost passed out while I was doing it. Then she took some pain-easing tablets I'd got and I left her curled up on the back seat. I guessed she'd pretty soon fall asleep, and I was hoping she'd stay that way until I'd met up with Garvin.

It was gonna be a long, hard drive. I put my cigarettes handy where I could get at them without much trouble, turned up the collar of my coat and settled myself behind the wheel. I was gonna have to shift to make up all the time Garvin had made on us.

I got her up to the 60 mark and kept my foot down so that we cruised at that speed. The telegraph poles slipped away, the long ribbon of road unfolded in front of me. I passed sleepy little villages with a rush that almost took them along with me. Once a huge lorry came out from a bend well over on my side of the road with blazing headlights glaring full in my eyes. I only just managed to get out of that. One wheel went up on the bank and a fence scraped the paint off my fender. It made my nerves tauten up, but I didn't relax speed.

It must have been four in the morning when I pulled up 20 yards past a filling station. I pulled past deliberately so as nobody calling in would see Joel stretched out on the back seat.

I got a coupla cans of steaming hot tea and some sandwiches.

Joel woke up long enough to get some heat inside her, but the tablets were the right stuff and she dropped off to sleep again. Lying there, with a wisp of hair lying across her cheek and her lips gently parted, she looked so calm and serene it was hard to believe all that she'd gone through.

Then I started off again. Joel had told me exactly where the place was and pretty soon, just as dawn began to break, I saw we hadn't far to go. Signposts along the way were ticking off the mileage.

I crested a hill, and in the morning light I saw a long way ahead of me a car at the side of the road. As I drew near, three figures spread themselves out across the road and waved for me to stop. I slowed down and was almost on top of them before I recognised Froggie, who'd grabbed Joel on the beach. A quick glance at the other two showed Garvin and Slit-mouth Joe. Without thinking, I pressed hard on the accelerator and flashed straight at them. Froggie was a bit slow. My wing caught him and tossed him across the road. Thirty yards further on, I stopped.

They'd recognised Gwen's car and they came running, shooting as they came.

One slug smashed the back window and another ricocheted off the coachwork before I realised what a sucker I was for stopping. I belted off again at top speed, having learnt one thing. Garvin's car had a tyre missing. He'd be a while catching up on me. I had a chance to get to Blondie and get her and Joel away. Then I could sit back and wait for Garvin to turn up. I knew he'd come right enough.

11

Twenty-odd miles further along, acting on the instructions Joel had already given me, I turned left off the high road and took a second-class road leading to a dump called Routinedene. After we'd left Routinedene behind us, I followed along a lane that was barely wide enough for two cars to pass for another five miles and found a wood on my left, just as Joel had said I would. I slowed down to about ten miles an hour, crawling along like that until I came to a farm track winding through the woods.

I thought it was gonna be too tough on the car. It wasn't my car and I was willing to drive her until she fell to bits. But every now and again we'd slip into a muddy pothole and the back wheels spun madly until they bit into firmer ground. Then at last the track through the woods opened out onto a glade and there, set like an island in a lake, was the log hut where Blondie was staying.

I drove right over to the door, lurching over the rough grass with my finger pressed down hard on the hooter. I vaguely realised it was early in the morning to be calling, but at a time like this I wasn't worrying about etiquette.

I switched off the engine, slammed outa the car, took the wooden steps up to the veranda two at a time and burst in through the double doors.

'Anybody at home?' I yelled.

There was the sound of a door opening upstairs and then Blondie's startled face looked over the landing.

'Put your skates on sister,' I yelled, 'you're getting outa here.'

'What?'

I was forgetting she hadn't had time to figure what I was doing that time in the morning.

'No time for questions, sister. Get dressed quick if you wanna stay healthy.'

She came down the stairs, cautiously. I noticed she had one hand in the pocket of her negligee. It may have contained a gun. I didn't know and I didn't care.

'What are you doing here?' she demanded.

'Don't pull that on me. You know who I am.'

She'd got to the bottom of the stairs by this time. She kept her distance from me, and there was no doubt about what was in her pocket now. She didn't need to draw a diagram to prove I was covered.

'Put that gun away and get wise. I haven't come all the way here, driving all night in order to argue. Dash upstairs, Blondie, and start ...'

I broke off because I suddenly realised we had company.

It was a long, lean-faced merchant with bushy eyebrows and a Gary Cooper manner about the way he had draped himself over the landing banisters. He was wearing a dressing gown, too.

I looked at him and I looked at Blondie. Then I looked at him again.

Casually he undraped himself from the banisters, and with a cigarette drooping from the corner of his mouth he came slowly down the stairs. Not once did he take his eyes off me.

'Who's this fella?' he said to Blondie out of the corner of his mouth.

'Some crazy guy who's been following me around.'

'You crazy bitch,' I said to her. 'Does everybody have to have a sex interest in order to do things. I came here to get you out of trouble ...'

'Out,' jerked Gary Cooper. He thumbed towards the door and took a step towards me. I looked at him and measured him up. He was a tough prospect, I figured.

'Call this dope off, Blondie,' I said. 'I've gotta talk to you.'

I should have been watching him instead of Blondie. He didn't like being called a dope. He led to my guts with his left, and if his calculations had been good he'd have kneed my chin as I doubled up. But he was too slow. I gave with the punch and caught him a beauty square on the point of his jaw. He staggered back on his heels so far, I thought he'd never recover his balance. The wall saved him. He stood there as if he couldn't believe it had happened, shook his head twice to clear it and then catapulted at me. I shoved up my mitts, but it was like trying to stop a bull with a paper hoop. He hit my hands, my hands bounced back on my chin and I went backwards over a chair.

Before I'd recovered my breath, he had me by the throat and was choking me. I didn't like it. I showed him I didn't like it. He was astride me and I kicked upwards, through his legs. My toe contacted with the base of his spine. It was a kick that would fell a horse. He went limp and collapsed on top of me.

I wriggled out from underneath and gently massaged my throat.

'I told you to call him off,' I said.

Blondie didn't answer. She was fondling him and saying tweety-dovey things as if that would bring him round.

'Listen, Blondie,' I said. 'Leave that crackerjack alone for a minute, will ya. Don't take my word for anything. Joel's asleep in the back of the car. Just go out and have a look at her back and remember that your pal Garvin did it. Then come back and do as I say.'

The name Garvin startled her. She looked at me with an expression of fear in her eyes. 'Garvin–' she gasped. 'Joel ...'

She almost ran across the room and down the steps.

Gary Cooper was fluttering his eyelids. I took a poker from the fireplace and stood over him. A few moments later his glazed eyes opened. He looked around dimly and then he looked at me and the glaze cleared.

'Why, you little runt ...' he said, as he began to get up. I waved the poker menacingly. He got the idea and lay back again.

'I'm not asking for trouble, kid,' I told him. 'But I sure can dish it out. And I can dish it out good, especially with a tool like this.' I toyed with the poker.

He just looked without saying anything; Gary Cooper stuff again.

At that moment Blondie came in. There was a set, determined expression on her face.

'Stop the tough stuff, Larry,' she ordered. ' Joel's outside in the car. Get her in here, and careful how you do it.'

Larry looked at me. He looked at the poker.

' I don't wanna get tough,' I said. 'I just want a little co-operation around here. You gonna play ball?'

'I can save it till later,' he grunted.

I let him up and we went out together and carried Joel in carefully. When Larry saw the weals on her back his eyebrows lowered and his lips grew tight, but he didn't ask questions.

Blondie got busy with creams and oils.

'Ya gotta hurry, Blondie,' I said. 'Garvin'll be here any minute now. Ya gotta get outa here.'

'What's the matter?' she said, gently rubbing oil into raw flesh. 'Are you yella?'

'I came here for just one reason. To get you away before Garvin gets here. This time it's you he's after. He'll never let you outa here alive.'

'Let him come,' she said calmly.

Larry butted in. 'Is this Garvin guy the fella what's been holding a torch for you and bumping off people?'

'Yes, Larry,' she said quietly.

'I think I'll hang around, too.'

'You're crazy,' I said. 'He's got his thugs with him. You don't stand an earthly.'

'How many guns have we got upstairs?' she asked Larry quietly.

'There's four that we use for deer-stalking. But you're gonna do like this fella says, Blondie. You're gonna get outa here quick.'

She chuckled. 'Not this babe. This is the showdown. Garvin's caused enough harm and trouble.' Her face hardened as she looked at Joel's back. A tear crept down her cheek. 'This has got to stop.'

'I'll take care of it,' said Larry.

'No,' she said. 'It's my party.'

'I guess we can move you by force,' said Larry.

'It's my party,' she said. 'It's gotta be done my way.'

Then she suddenly flared at us. 'I gotta see it done myself. I love that guy. Hell, I love him so I can't live without him.' She broke off into uncontrollable sobs that shook her through and through.

It made me feel uncomfortable. I looked at Larry, he looked at me and shrugged his shoulders.

I walked over to the window. 'This hut's in a clearing.'

'Yeah,' said Larry. 'Makes it kinda difficult for folks you're expecting to get on top of you before you know about it.'

'Two guns at the front and one at the back would make it kinda difficult for callers,' I agreed.

Larry went upstairs. Blondie finished her good Samaritan work and made some coffee.

Larry came down again with the guns under his arm and boxes of cartridges. Quite calmly we began to barricade the windows and the doors with mattresses and bits of furniture.

The effects of the sleeping tablets wore off and Joel woke up under the ministrations of warm coffee. The poor kid looked white and tired, but she worked up a smile for us all, and there was that sparkle in her wide eyes that always got me.

The time passed without excitement. Larry sat over by the window, a cigarette drooping from his mouth, Joel lay stretched out on the divan with her head in my lap, and Blondie made up her face and combed her hair.

'Going somewhere, kid?' I jeered.

'It's my party,' she reminded.

'The guests need a drink.'

Blondie got a bottle of Rye and splashed out a good measure all round.

I began to be aware of the clock on the wall, ticking. None of us was talking. There was a kind of suspense in the air. With a shock, I realised that I was feeling like I did just before we went into action.

'Hank,' said Joel. She squeezed my hand. I squeezed back. 'Is it gonna be all right?'

'Sure,' I said confidently. I should have known then. I always feel that way just before things I don't like begin to happen. But I never realise it until after they've happened. There was a strange sense of unreality. Deep down at the back of my subconscious mind was the feeling that I'd been through all this before.

'Everything is going to be all right, Hank,' she insisted.

'There's not a thing to worry about, honey.'

She was quiet after that, and I could hear that damn clock ticking again. Blondie poured out some more Scotch and Larry eased himself from one side of the window to the other. There was a ring of cigarette ends around him.

The clock went on ticking. Larry picked up his gun.

'They're coming,' he said quietly.

I went over to the other window. It was a couple of hundred yards to the woods, and four figures were stumbling towards us over the rough ground. It was too far to pick them out.

I picked up my rifle and waited. As they approached, I could pick out Nat. Froggy was unmistakable because of his girth. Joe, the man who'd slugged me on the beach, and the other fella looked pretty much alike.

I waited.

Larry waited.

Blondie spoilt it by letting off too soon. Just the sort of daft thing a dame will do. She upped with her gun and let fly. One of the figures, it could have been Joe, clapped a hand to his shoulder, and then all of them turned and ran for the woods.

I looked at Larry. He didn't say anything. He just spat and lit another cigarette.

I knew what he was thinking. They'd been sitting birds. Another hundred yards and we could have picked them off. Those that had run for it, if we had missed, we could have picked off at our leisure.

Now they knew what they were up against and they'd play canny.

'Did I do it wrong?' said Blondie. In her woman's way, she'd detected a certain coldness in our manner.

'That's all right, kid,' said Larry. 'You done fine.' He added something under his breath, but Blondie didn't catch it

'What d'you think they'll do next?' she asked.

'Circle around and try from the back,' said Larry. He reloaded Blondie's gun. 'Up to you,' he said to me, and went through to the back.

I stood in the angle of the window and looked across to the woods. I couldn't see any movements. I leaned forward and looked out the other way, and a bullet smashed the glass above my head and covered me in splinters.

I ducked down quicker than greased lightning.

Joel came running over to me. I pulled her down on top of me just before the bullets started thudding again.

'Are you crazy?' I asked.

'Darling, darling, I thought you were hurt.'

I brushed my cheeks against her lips while she clung to me.

'I'll wake you up when they get here,' rapped Blondie coldly.

'All right, smartie,' I replied.

I kissed Joel again and took another gander through the window. There wasn't a movement.

I waited.

Blondie waited.

It was so quiet that we could hear Larry strike a match out the back.

That damned clock went on ticking.

'Hold my hand,' said Joel.

I didn't mind that a bit. It hadn't been like that out East. There hadn't been anybody to hold the boys' hands then, and you can bet your boots they'd have liked it.

Blondie tossed a packet of cigarettes across to me. I lit two with one match and passed one cigarette to Joel. She squeezed my hand and nuzzled me. Her cheek pressed against mine.

'Darling,' I said.

We were so close I could feel her heart beating, a gentle flutter against my breast.

Larry suddenly began to fire, steadily and rapidly. I could tell from the steady pause while he reloaded that he was firing coolly and scientifically.

There was nothing moving on my side.

Larry stopped firing after a while.

'What happened?' I called.

I heard the rasp of a match. 'They tried rushing me,' he reported. 'I winged one. He's still there, trying to crawl back.'

A few seconds later he fired once more.

'They rushing you again?' I called.

'No,' said Larry coolly and with meaning.

That meant there were now only three of them to deal with. They might decide to wait for reinforcements. On the other hand they might go away altogether.

Another half-hour passed slowly. The sun was beginning to come up and it was gonna be hot. I untied my necktie and opened my shirt.

'There's something going on,' said Blondie.

There was, too. They'd manoeuvred their car up to the edge of the woods. It was facing us and something about the way it was placed struck a cord in my memory. With one sweep of my hand I shoved Joel flat on the floor.

'Duck, Blondie,' I yelled. 'Flat on the floor.'

It was hell while it lasted. They'd got a typewriter fixed on the side of the car and it was a speedy model. Lead smashed against and through the walls of the shack, cutting from side to side. Overhead the pictures, ornaments, crockery and furniture danced around like wild things, and glass, china and wood splinters flew across the room.

It lasted almost a minute.

When it stopped, Larry called out to us.

'All okay in here,' I reported.

I knew the gag. 'Everybody keep down,' I ordered.

Two or three minutes passed and then another burst of lead pulverised us. Blondie began to look a little scared.

I got round to the side of the window and squinted out. I waited about five minutes and then they came running. They'd spread themselves out, attacking from three directions at the same time.

I'd have picked them off nice and pretty if it hadn't been for that damn Blondie. She opened out again and they went scuttling back. I threw a few shots after them, but I knew it was too long a shot.

'How you making out?' called Larry.

I was risking my head watching them, but they weren't worrying about me. I saw what they were up to and it got me worried.

'Better come in, Larry,' I called.

He came in on hands and knees. He didn't want a gutful of lead thrown at him.

'They're gonna rush us with the car.'

'Yeah.' He looked interested.

We reloaded rapidly, loosened up our spare cartridges. Larry lit another cigarette.

'What d'you think of their chances? '

I didn't answer him. I was beginning to think that Blondie was the cause of a whole lot of trouble, and it stood a good chance of being the beginning of the end as things were.

'Keep low until we have to get up,' I told Larry.

He spat on the floor. Gary Cooper to the last, I thought.

And then they came. As soon as the car started charging across the grass towards us, the typewriter opened up.

We lay there, listening to the sound of the frantically-accelerated engine picking up top speed and the whine and tear of bullets.

It was like being dive-bombed. Lead thudded all around us, eating through the walls, spraying devastation everywhere. I yelled in agony as a ricochet bullet slammed into my thigh.

Larry gave one look at me. Bullets were still cutting

the air around us. He gave a drag at his fag, stubbed it out and then coolly stood up and levelled his rifle.

I saw the gun kick against his shoulder almost at the same time as his head smashed back. He fell face upwards with the neatest, cleanest hole in his forehead you could ever expect to see.

Almost at the same moment, the car smashed into the veranda, ploughed through it and jammed with its nose embedded in the door. I kneeled up in time to see Froggie let go the back of the car and come charging towards us.

I think Blondie and I both got him at the same time. He went down like a log, not even kicking.

Then there was that kind of silence that always comes in the numbed interval between a happening and the realisation that it has happened.

Gingerly I peeked over the windowsill. Slit-mouth Joe was hunched over the wheel of the car. Otherwise there wasn't a sign of anybody apart from Froggie, and I didn't need to worry about him.

'Where's Nat?' said Blondie.

'Hadn't the guts,' I guessed.

She looked down at Larry. 'Just one more,' she said quietly. She was all tied up inside, I could tell that. This dame sure was death to anyone who knew her. And she knew it.

And then for the first time the pain from my leg came up and hit me. At first there had been the force of the impact and then a strange numbness that was frightening. And now came the pain in great, heavy waves that made me want to shriek my head off.

I gripped my hands so tight that the nails lacerated the palms of my hands. The sweat stood out in great drops on my forehead, and a low moan forced itself through my clenched teeth.

Joel rolled back my trouser leg. I heard the quick intake of her breath as she saw the wound, and then she got busy with scissors, cutting my trousers away.

'It's not too bad, darling,' she said, soft fingers working deftly. 'It's clean. The bullet's gone right through. Only it's bleeding a great deal.'

I got fingers and thumb above the wound and pressed hard. 'Get a handkerchief and a piece of wood,' I instructed.

She tied the handkerchief around my thigh, above the wound, and I passed a piece of wood between the handkerchief and my leg and twisted it round. It was a rough tourniquet but it served its purpose. When it was real tight, I fixed the wood so it wouldn't get loose, and Joel got a bandage on me.

After that I felt I wanted a cigarette.

Blondie was standing up and looking out of the window.

'I can't see Nat,' she said.

'Them kinda guys are always yella,' I said. 'He sends his boys to run the risks, but he don't take chances himself.'

'It's not like him,' said Blondie, thoughtfully.

She checked her rifle carefully, then rested it against the wall. Then she pulled a little pearl-handled pistol from her dressing-gown pocket and checked that.

'Have you used it yet?' I asked.

'Not yet,' she said in tones that suggested she expected she would soon.

'What now?' asked Joel.

'Yeah, what now?' I said.

'Nat will come,' said Blondie. ' I know him, he'll be here.'

'He'll get another six toughs together first,' I guessed.

Blondie leaned forward and looked out of the window again. Something made me look up, and for a moment I was gagging.

On the landing overlooking us was Nat Garvin. He must have taken advantage of the turmoil when the car smashed into the shack to clamber up over the roof and climb in through a window.

He had his gun in his hand and was just bringing it to bear on Blondie.

It was as though the vocal cords in my throat had snapped. For an eternity I sat there and watched Garvin, before I found my voice.

'Blondie,' I yelled. ' Behind you, look out!'

She must have been on tiptoe. Even as I yelled she began to turn, and the little revolver she held lifted up and spurted flame. At the same time, Garvin's gun barked. Blondie spun round like a top and flopped on the floor. Her little revolver went skidding across the room.

Garvin stood there a moment with his gun still smoking in his hand. He swayed slightly and his mouth fell open. Joel's nails dug into my arm.

It was like watching a picture. Garvin slowly doubled up over the banister. It was a low rail, and as he leaned over it the weight of his body carried him forward. He turned completely over before he hit the floor beneath with a thud that reverberated underneath me.

I thought he was a stiff. The fall alone must have pulped a good few bones. But Garvin wasn't done, yet.

He fell in a sitting position, his back against the wall, and by some miracle his gun was still in his hand

and still smoking. And then his eyes opened, dully reflecting the great blackness that was coming upon him. Slowly, painfully slowly, he lifted his hand, pressing for the pit of his stomach. Dark streaks of blood crawled over the backs of his fingers as he pressed his hand into his belly. His other hand lay lifeless at his side, fingers still clenched tightly around the butt of his gun.

A noise came from Blondie. An animal kind of grunt. I saw one white arm reach up and clutch at a tabletop. Slowly, painfully, an inch at a time, she pulled herself to her feet. Joel gasped and hid her face in my shoulder. I gasped too when I saw that Blondie's shoulder had been so badly smashed. Her arm hung limply gew-gaw, streams of blood ran down her arm and dripped from her fingertips and splinters of white bone were sticking out from her smashed shoulder.

I didn't think it possible for anyone to still be conscious smashed up that way.

But there was a strange, fixed expression on Blondie's face. Leaning heavily on the table, she took one faltering step forward. Her eyes were fixed on the little revolver lying on the floor a few yards from her. It must have seemed a million miles away. She made another faltering step and almost collapsed. With an effort she recovered. After that she was on her own. There was nothing to hold onto. She took one more step, and then quite slowly and deliberately Garvin raised his gun. He was too far gone to take aim. Without looking, he just lifted his gun arm and fired.

The slug smashed into Blondie's hip, knocking her flat. The sound alone of lead smashing bone was enough to make me sick. The whole of her side became one dripping mass of mashed flesh and bone.

And then the incredible happened. It made me

want to cry out aloud and laugh hysterically at the time. I couldn't believe it was happening.

Blondie's head came up. She looked at Garvin and she looked at the gun lying on the floor a bare yard from her, and then somehow she dragged her suffering, bleeding body an inch forward. The expression in Garvin's eyes didn't change. He just watched as, inch by inch, somehow pulling herself forward, Blondie edged closer and closer to the gun.

Her hand was nine inches from the gun, six inches, four inches …

Garvin was making an effort. His mouth worked as he tried to speak, the muscles of his gun arm jerked. Blood trickled from the corner of his mouth as waveringly his gun arm lifted. Joel caught her breath.

I suddenly remembered that I still had a gun in my pocket. I began to fumble for it. It was caught underneath me and I couldn't get at it.

Garvin's gun wavered, levelled, wavered and then spat flame. The slug cut right alongside Blondie's face, cutting a groove across her cheek that spurted blood and carried away part of her ear. But her fingers still groped, closed around the butt of the gun.

Slowly, without emotion, Garvin's eyes switched around to me as I still fumbled with the trigger guard caught in the lining of my pocket. His gun swung around to bear on me, and Joel screamed.

She flung herself across my body just as Garvin fired. I actually heard the bullet smack into her back. She gave a kinda grunt, 'Aaaar,' and I guess I went kinda mad.

This just couldn't be happening to me. It was too much to stand. Everything revolved around me. In my subconscious mind I heard other shots, but they didn't mean anything.

Joel was in my arms, her full weight lying on my wounded leg so that pain screeched through me from top to toe. Over and over and over again I was hearing the soft plunk of lead smashing into her. I was holding her tight, pressing her to me.

'Hold me tight, Hank,' she whispered. Her eyes were wide, staring at me with a frightened expression deep at the back of them.

'Joel,' I moaned, 'Joel.' I clutched her tighter. It seemed I couldn't get close enough to her. I wanted to be so close to her that we were one.

Tears gathered at the corner of her eyes. 'Hank,' she whispered again. 'Don't let me go. Don't let me go, I'm frightened.'

Her eyes fluttered. Waves of agony swept through me, the room began to revolve again, and through a haze I heard her voice. 'Hank, don't let me go, don't let me go.'

'I've got you, honey. I won't let you go,' I tried to say, but the words wouldn't form themselves. The treacly black thickness was upon me again, a whirring sound in my ears that was rapidly getting louder and louder. My senses were slipping from me, and I struggled against the waves of dark agony swooping down at me.

Through a blur, I heard her moan my name over and over again before I slipped down and away from everything.

12

I didn't want to wake up ever again. I fought against it, pushing wakefulness away from me with my subconscious. But when the strong afternoon sun did force its way through my eyelids and I blinked against the light, I knew with a sickness that was embedded in my guts why I didn't want to wake up.

I knew immediately my eyes opened, and for that reason I wouldn't shift my eyes from the ceiling. I must have lain there a long time like that before I summoned up the courage to do the thing I hated to do.

She was like a sleeping child. It helped, her being like that, smiling quietly with her eyes closed as if she'd just slipped off into a doze.

I edged her gently away from me, lifted her from off my leg and sucked in my breath with the sudden stab of pain it caused.

I didn't want to kiss her or anything like that. I just looked at her and then tried to choke back the misery that came bubbling up in my throat. Then gingerly I got up, using the windowsill as a support.

The room was a shambles and there was a kinda deathly silence that hushed everything. I tried slowly putting weight on my bad leg. It throbbed, but it took my weight. Slowly I hobbled across to what was left of Blondie. She'd caused her last deaths. She'd managed to get to her revolver. It was still clenched tight in her fingers, and when my eyes automatically travelled to Nat, there was nothing but a big hole in his chest, showing that even at the end Blondie had grouped her shots well.

I grabbed the decanter and tilted myself a humdinger Scotch. It took three gulps to get it down, and after that I gasped for breath for some minutes while the tingling ran right down from my throat to my toes.

Then I hobbled through to the kitchen, got a bowl of water and sat down.

I was dreading what I was going to see when I got the bandage off my leg. And it took a load off my mind to see what a nice clean hole it was, entrance and exit marked clearly and no signs of any broken bones.

I cleaned it up thoroughly, using raw spirits as an antiseptic, and then bound it up with strips from a teacloth I found hanging up. Then I gargled, rinsed my face in cold water and felt a helluva lot better. That is as long as I could stop thinking about Joel.

I had just found a packet of fags and was lighting up when I heard the noise of a car drawing up. Automatically I got out the gun I had in my pocket and edged over to the door of the living room.

It was Gwen. She came busting in, gave one look towards Nat and then began to scream hysterically.

I waited to see who was with her. She went on screaming and sobbing to herself for some minutes and no-one else showed up. I eased myself around the doorjamb and stood there quietly, waiting.

After a while she turned off the waterworks. When she saw me she gave a jump of surprise and her eyes flew to the gun I was holding in my hand. But I didn't need to tell her what had happened.

'Blondie killed him?' There was a break in her voice, and the question was really a statement.

'He had it coming,' I said brutally. I hadn't any sympathy for Garvin.

'No-one ever understood him,' she said.

'Nobody except you,' I suggested mockingly.

She sank down into a chair, the back of which had been eaten away by bullets, twisting a handkerchief in her hands.

I tossed a packet of cigarettes in her lap and poured her a drink.

'What am I going to do now?'

She had become suddenly pathetic, alone, lost.

'You'll be much better off, honey,' I reassured her. 'The Golden Peacock will be yours, and that's a classy joint. It'll hang a few diamond bracelets around your neck each year.'

'But what about this?' She swept her arm around her.

I knew what she meant. The cops would have described it as four dead bodies inside the house and three outside. They'd start hunting around for clues and evidence and in no time there'd be a first class enquiry, involving every citizen who ever set foot inside Garvin's joint, including me.

I did a little quiet thinking.

'Gwen,' I said at last. 'You got any superstitions about burial? I mean, do you object to cremation?'

She looked at me in surprise. 'Say, when a guy's dead, he's dead, isn't he? He don't make no croak about

117

the worms, the lime or the flames getting him. I guess it's all the same to him.'

'That's the way I figure things, Gwen. Now listen carefully. We're gonna have all this cleaned up, see? We don't want no trouble, no traces left, no evidence. Nothing. See?'

'You mean, burn this joint down?'

'Yep.'

She thought that over and then said, 'What about Nat's car? It's smashed up outside.'

'We'll take off the number-plates. Take them away with us. It'll burn with the hut.'

'And the fellas outside?'

'That, my dear Gwen, is gonna be your toughest job. They gotta be brought in here. But with this leg of mine, it ain't gonna be easy. You gotta help.'

She swallowed hard. 'Okay,' she said. 'Let's get it over quick.'

It wasn't a pleasant job. Froggy didn't look too good normally. He looked much less inviting with half his face blown away. Joe had gone stiff at the driving wheel and we had to carry him in a sitting position. It made me sweat, and Gwen was white-faced.

'There's still one more,' I told her.

She was toughening up by this time. 'Leave it to me,' she told me, and while I began to take off the number-plates on Garvin's car she ran her own car across the grass at the back, slipped a rope around the fella's body and dragged him to the hut, hooked onto the back bumper.

I began to swill petrol over the floor. There were spare cans in the back of Garvin's car, and in Gwen's car, too. I made a good job of it, and somehow, in some strange way, I felt I was building a funeral pyre to the honour of Joel.

'Better run through Nat's pockets, see if there's any means of identification.'

Gwen turned out all his pockets, took rings off his fingers.

I frisked the others. There wasn't more than a handful of stuff that might have meant anything. That we could throw away later.

I opened all the windows to make a good draught, stood over by the door and threw in a match. It went up with a loud *whoof* that almost took off my eyebrows. In three minutes there was a blaze going that Niagara couldn't have quenched.

'What now?' said Gwen.

'We beat it,' I told her, 'before the local sheriff and fire brigade come along to see what's doing.'

My leg was still giving me hell. I climbed into the cream and green limousine and Gwen sat at the controls. We bumped across the grass onto the rough track through the woods. Behind us the log hut was dissolving into a funnel of smoke that would be seen for miles.

'Hold it,' I said suddenly. Gwen jammed on the brakes.

'How did you get here?' I asked her.

'Hire car. It's parked just back there.'

'Jeezus,' I said.

'Well, what's wrong with that?' she asked challengingly.

'It's like leaving your visiting card.'

'Yeah, so it is.' She said that after having thought about it for a minute.

'Listen, dumb girl, go back and get that car and drive it in front of me. Head north. I'll follow. I want 50 or 60 miles between us and here before we stop. D'you understand?'

'But your leg,' she protested. 'You can't drive with your leg in that shape.'

'Get along,' I almost shouted at her. She looked at me for a moment and then got out of the car and ran back up the path.

I edged over to the driver's seat and tested my foot on the controls. Jagged flames of fire ran up my leg. I gritted my teeth.

A few minutes later she nosed into the mirror reflection over the dashboard. I waved her on. She got past me in that narrow path, just missing scraping the paint off my wing, and then she was off. I let in the clutch and followed, clenching my hands tight on the steering wheel and fighting back the waves of nausea flowing from my wound to my head. Every time the car bumped over a pothole, I almost went out through the roof with the excruciating agony of the jarring, and I just didn't seem to be able to miss those potholes.

We played follow-my-leader right through the woods and back onto the main road. Gwen opened up then to a steady 50, and I kept right behind on her tail. After a while she signalled she was slowing down. I came up alongside.

'What say we dump this car here?' she said. 'Cripes, you've got a face like a cold cod on a wet slab. That leg must be eating you.'

The leg *was* eating me. I could feel my forehead dewed with the sweat of pain. I wasn't surprised I looked white.

'Get going,' I gritted at her. 'Don't stop till I hoot.'

'Okay,' she said, 'it's your party.'

As we set off again, I turned her words over and

over in my mind. 'My party,' she'd called it. Blondie had called it her party. But that hadn't stopped Joel getting a slug right in her back. I jerked my mind away from that line of thought. It didn't get me nowhere.

Lola hadn't got anywhere either. She'd finished up with a slug in her back too. But it was worthwhile knowing that Garvin was finished, and that he'd taken some of his hired gunmen with him.

I kept my eye on the back of Gwen's car. My leg wasn't paining anymore. It was just numb. The numbness was slowly creeping through my leg. I couldn't feel the controls at all. When I pressed down, I could tell the clutch was thrown out, but I couldn't feel the pedal.

We drove on like that mile after mile, town after town. The signposts slipped away behind us and my indicator had clocked 85 miles before I hooted. Gwen slowed down immediately.

I handed her a pencil. 'Let the air outa one of the tyres,' I instructed.

'Say, what good is that gonna ...?'

'Shut your trap and do what I say.'

I felt too weak to explain everything in detail, and Gwen had enough gumption not to argue. She let out the air in a back tyre, and when it was right flat I said:

'Now, I don't want any mistakes. Drive on to the next garage. Pull in there and say you've got a flat. Get a bit frantic because you're short of time.' I gave her other instructions and then watched as she drove off.

The car wobbled like a lame duck. Gwen got up speed and I followed a good way behind. Shreds of the tyre got left on the road. When eventually I saw her pull into a garage, the tyre must have been almost off.

I waited a few minutes and then sped up to the

garage, swung in and pulled up with a squeal of brakes.

'Fill her up and make it snappy,' I told the mechanic.

Gwen came running over, clip-clopping on high-heeled shoes, skirt way up above her knees. The car was up on the ramp and a coupla mechanics were busy on it.

'Hi, mister,' she called. I looked around. 'Can you take me along with you? I'm late for a date. It's terribly important.' Gwen would have made a good actress. There was desperate entreaty in her voice and only a flint-heart could have refused.

'Hop in,' I told her.

She climbed in, and as we drove off she yelled instructions to the mechanic to keep the car until it was phoned for.

A coupla miles down the road, I pulled up.

'Gonna take over now?' I asked.

'Sure. Just slide over. I'll get in the other side.'

As she opened the door the side where I'd been sitting, she stopped suddenly and stared at the floor.

I knew what she was looking at. My boot was full of blood.

She climbed in and said determinedly, 'Better let me look at that leg.'

'Leave it,' I said. 'Wait till I get back.'

'I'm not driving an inch till I've seen that leg.'

'Okay,' I said.

We got the bandages off. They were soaked with blood and useless.

'What have you got for a fresh bandage?'

I shrugged. There wasn't anything I could think of.

'Get your tie off,' she instructed.

'That's not gonna be much help.'

'Do what I say.'

I shrugged again and began to undo my tie. Gwen began fumbling underneath her skirt. Then she lifted her fanny off the seat, wriggled, and a few seconds later slid delicate, rose-petal panties down her legs. She folded them into a small, hard pad and bound them around my leg with my tie.

'Now you'll catch cold,' I said.

'Nuts,' she replied.

I fainted soon after that.

It was dark when I came around. Gwen was driving furiously.

'There's Scotch in the pocket,' she said, not taking her eyes off the road.

I felt in the pocket and got the stopper off the bottle.

I felt better after I'd had a swig. I passed it to her and she tipped some into her mouth.

'Be home in half an hour,' she said.

'Yeah.'

'Get you to bed.'

'Yeah, I could do with some of that.' I moved my leg and it was still there. I touched it with my fingers and made sure about it.

'How's it go?' she asked.

'Still on,' I replied. 'Wanna keep it if I can.'

Soon the outskirts of town were racing past us and then it was a short cry to my apartments. I was glad that it was so early. The neighbours had seen me come home with a blanket around me. I wasn't anxious to wave a bloodstained trouser-leg at them.

'I'll come up with you,' said Gwen.

I edged out of the car, balanced on one leg and

tentatively extended the other before me. It held all right. Gwen slipped my arm around her shoulder and together we climbed the stairs to the front door. I couldn't remember where I'd put my keys, but Gwen found them in my jacket pocket. After that it was a slow, painful ascent up three long flights of tenement stairs. I breathed a sigh of relief when I was able to stretch out on my bed.

'I'll fix that leg again for you,' said Gwen.

I was pretty hazy. I watched her bustle around getting towels and water and felt her fumble with the bandages. I'd lost a lot of blood and was noticing it. Pretty soon I hazed into a deep sleep. I was lying there with Gwen holding my hand, and then Garvin and his hoodlums all crowded into the room and began to leer at me. I jumped off the bed and told 'em to get the hell outa it. Garvin laughed and snapped his fingers. Immediately everyone dissolved into flames, little jets of flame that licked upwards around the curtains, along the carpets.

I rushed and threw a pail of water over everything, but it was petrol, not water, and the flames grew stronger and stronger, smoke clogged my throat and outside I beard the fire-bells ringing, ringing, ringing, ringing. They rang so long they woke me up. I lay there for some minutes trying to remember where I was, and all the time the telephone went on ringing urgently.

I cradled the receiver. 'Who is it?'

'You Janson?'

'So what?' It was a voice I didn't recognise.

'D'you know Gwen Garvin?'

Apprehension thrilled through me.

'Yeah,' I said.

'She slipped me a message. Says she's in trouble at the Golden Peacock. Wants you to get down there right away.'

I sat up on the bed and nursed that information for a bit. Then I got up slowly, limped to the bathroom and ducked my head under the tap. It was late afternoon. I'd been sleeping for hours.

It took a long time, but I changed my trousers and grabbed another necktie. Somehow I'd still managed to hang onto a gun. I kept that in my pocket. When I looked at myself in the mirror, I didn't look any great shakes. But I could walk and that was something.

I limped down the stairs and stood on the kerb till I could flag a taxi.

Everything seemed to be happening all over again. But this time it was different, because Garvin was out. He was a dead duck.

I went in the front entrance of the Golden Peacock and allowed the head waiter to show me to a table. When the cabaret started I got up and limped around to the door marked 'Office.'

As soon as it opened I had my good foot in the gap and my rod levelled at Hare-lip's midriff. He didn't argue. He opened up like a good boy and let me through.

I took him up in the lift with me the same as before. It was like a dream gone wild, reality repeating reality. When the lift-gates opened I shoved Hare-lip well to the fore to meet the reception boys. But there was none waiting.

I gunned Hare-lip along in front of me towards Garvin's room, just exactly as I'd done it before – and – and then came the difference.

It was a gun muzzle thrust hard against my spine.

'Keep those mitts well up.'

I shoved my mitts up.

'Okay, Hare-lip, get downstairs again.'

Hare-lip scuttled off and I was marched along to Garvin's room. Acting as instructed, I opened the door, and then a rough thrust sent me sprawling on the carpet. I winced as the muscles in my leg were torn and the wound broken open again.

When I looked up it was to see the two men who'd previously had the pleasure of my company. They both had me covered. There was a third, tall man there with Gwen.

I looked hard at Gwen.

'I didn't tell them anything,' she protested.

'Shut your trap,' growled the tall man.

He slowly took a gun outa his pocket and trained it on my face.

'All right, get out, the lotta you,' he growled.

The others began to shuffle out.

'Not you,' he said to Gwen.

She stayed, and then when the door was closed behind the others, he said:

'So, smart guy, you put the finger on Nat, did you?'

I looked at Gwen again.

'I had to tell him,' she said. 'Hank, believe me, I had to tell him.'

'Dames have got big traps,' he told me. 'An' I'm thanking you, fella, for dropping everything in my lap.' He sprinkled ash from his cigarette over the carpet. 'Getting Garvin out of the way makes things easy for me. I've been wanting to run this set-up for quite a while.'

'What's that to me?'

'I'm just gonna rub you out,' he said calmly. 'One way and another I reckon you and your lady friend here know too much.'

'Phil,' cried Gwen. There was shock and surprise in her voice.

'Yeah, you too,' he said with a sudden snarl. 'There's only three people know what's happened to Nat. When I bump you two, there's only gonna be me left. And I won't talk. I'll just take over and manage things.' He leered confidently. 'Nat will be sending me instructions privately. That's what I'll tell the boys. And when I'm properly in the chair, I'll put it out that Nat's in the can, gone down for a lifer.'

'Phil,' cried Gwen. It was more of a scream than anything. For the first time in her life she was facing up to death that threatened *her*. She didn't like it any more than I did.

I guess it drove her cuckoo. She rushed at Phil, oblivious of his rod, and the very suddenness of it took him by surprise. He was too late to use his gun-arm except to send her flying backwards across the room with a clout to the jaw.

By that time I'd rolled behind the big table and got my own rod out. Half-lying, I fired around the edge of the table. It was a poor shot. It smashed into the wall above Phil's head. In one movement he dived behind the settee. A few seconds later a sliver of wood was cut from the table two inches above my head.

I was at home in this. I'd been in spots like this a dozen times out East. I slipped off my coat and edged it over the top of the desk. As a bullet clipped through it, I let fly round the side of the desk. My slug parted Phil's hair. He ducked down with a grunt.

After that I just waited. A minute ticked past.

'I can wait as long as you,' I said.

'Don't worry, Janson. You're in a spot.'

I guess we'd both forgotten about Gwen. She was an unconscious heap over in one corner.

Ten minutes passed with an occasional snap shot on either side making no score.

'How many slugs ya got left?' I asked.

He didn't answer. But I knew he'd get worried, because he didn't know how many I had.

And then there came the tramping of feet along the corridor. Heavy feet, big boots. A knock at the door.

'Who's there?' called Phil.

'The Law.' There was a long silence. 'Open up, will ya?'

'Better open up, Phil,' said another voice. 'This dick wants to have a talk with you.'

'Open the door. Phil,' I encouraged. 'This makes everything dandy. I can tell my piece. You'll go down for 20 years at least.'

'Open up!'

Gwen solved the deadlock. She must have recovered consciousness during this time. She suddenly ran across the room and began to unlock the door. It was just sheer madness. I guessed what she was doing as soon as she started to move, and when Phil came up to sling lead, I got him in the guts. But not before he'd fired. The slug went through the door six inches above her head. She got the door open at the same moment, and it swung in, forced open by the strong-arm cop who'd visited me. Only the cop wasn't pushing the door with his hands, he was leaning forward against it, because cops with bullets in the centre of their foreheads don't stand up without help.

At the same moment an alarm bell began to ring

on the desk. It went on ringing vibrantly.

'Jeezus,' whispered a fella outside. Then he took one look at me and went for his rod. I got him right off. Through the heart I guessed.

Gwen was standing in a kinda stupor, staring down at the copper. I shook her by the arm.

'What's that bell for?'

'Coppers,' she said. 'That's a raid signal.'

I shook her hard.

'We gotta get outa here,' I said.

'Yeah,' she said. 'I know a way.'

I edged over to the door and looked out. From downstairs came a sudden outburst of shooting. The corridor was deserted.

'This way,' said Gwen.

She led the way across the corridor, into a bedroom. There was a big closet there. She opened the door, pushed the dresses on one side and opened another door at the back of the closet. She switched on a light showing steps leading down. I followed her, slowly, limping.

When we got to the bottom, we walked along another corridor until we came to a blank door. There was a small attaché case at the door. Gwen picked it up.

'This is the back of a telephone kiosk,' explained Gwen. 'It opens out into a drugstore on the next corner.'

She looked through a little slit.

'Nobody's using the telephone. I'll go first, you follow afterwards.'

Cautiously she slid open the door and edged through. I followed, shutting the door behind me. It was a pretty tight squeeze. Then she opened the door of the kiosk and walked out through the shop. I followed, trying not to limp. A young jerk with horn-rimmed glasses and a glass of milk in front of him looked up from his study book and gazed at us with wonderment in his eyes. Then he looked at the telephone kiosk as if he couldn't believe his eyes. We didn't take any notice. We just walked on and out onto the street.

We stood on the kerb until a cab came and then we bundled inside.

'Where to?'

I gave him the address of my apartment.

'Did I hear shooting?' I asked. Squad cars were wailing their sirens along the road in the other direction.

'Yeah,' he said. 'Cops are raiding Garvin's joint.'

Gwen took my arm. I sank back on the upholstery.

'What do we do now?' she asked.

'You mean, what do you do.'

'Yeah, that's right.'

'You scram, sister. You get right outa town. If you've got any sense you won't come back. Once the cops have started on that joint they won't leave it until they've uncovered everything. Having that cop shot on the premises puts the finger on that joint. It's what the dicks have been wanting for a long, long time.'

'But Hank,' her voice was pleading. She tugged gently at my coat sleeve. 'Won't you come along with me?'

'You're big enough to go places by yourself.'

'But I'm scared, Hank. I'm scared of being alone. Won't you come too?'

'I'll give you a break,' I conceded. 'I'll run you out of town a short way.'

'Will you, Hank?'

I tapped on the window and told the driver to carry on to my garage. When we got there, Gwen got out, still grabbing tight to her attaché case, and I paid off the driver.

We got into my car and I drove. My leg was a lot better and I didn't want my gears torn to bits by a dame. Dames never can drive a car without wrenching its guts out unless they know the car well.

We didn't talk much, just sat there smoking. I was thinking that the score was just about clean now that the rest of Garvin's mob were being mopped up by the gendarmes. But where did that leave me? I still had to get a job of some kind.

'Hank,' said Gwen. There was a plaintive, little-girl approach in her tones.

'Hank,' she said. 'Couldn't we team up? I mean, we could carry on together. We've been through a lot together. I like you, too.'

'Naw,' I drawled. 'I ain't got no dough. I ain't got a future.'

'That's all right, Hank,' she said. 'I've got enough to carry on with.'

'It wouldn't work out.'

'Look, Hank,' she said. She opened the attaché case on her lap. I squinted at it sideways and nearly slewed across the road. The case was stacked with necklaces, diamonds and packets of dollar bills.

'Where d'you get that?'

'It was just around the place.' She laughed and shrugged. 'I guess we can get along for a while on that. Perhaps we could keep on travelling. Drive clean across the country. There's many states I've never seen. We aren't in any hurry, we can spend our time the way we like. If we hit a nice town, well we'll stop there a week, or a month, perhaps a year.'

It was a dazzling prospect. Having that dough behind us would give me a chance to get acclimatised. Perhaps we'd get a farm somewhere, keep hens or sows or something. And Gwen wasn't all that difficult to get on with, either. I wasn't unconscious of the meaningful way her knee was pressing against my leg.

'Okay, Gwen. It's a deal.'

'Fine. And now we haven't anything to think about except us. No more worries about what we've left behind.'

'Nope,' I said. 'But it was a close thing. If that cop hadn't turned up in time to have his brains leaded, we'd have been in a spot.

'Yeah,' I added thoughtfully. 'I wonder why those cops did come when they did?'

Gwen was smiling to herself.

'Did you have anything to do with it?' I was remembering the way that attaché case was ready and waiting for her in the secret passage. It looked like an arranged job.

'It was me,' she admitted.

'You got the cops in?'

'All by myself.'

'But how could you? Phil had you up in the room there.'

'I telephoned the cops before that.'

'Yeah?'

'Smart kid, aren't I?'

'Sure thing, Gwen. You're smarter than they come. What d'you tell the cops to make them come a-running the way they did?'

'I said there was a fella gonna be bumped ...'

She broke off suddenly and a scared look flitted

through her eyes. At the same time, I jammed on the brake and squealed to a halt. We were out in the country by this time and nobody was around.

'You told them what?' There was ice in my voice.

'I just told them that I thought there was gonna be some trouble among some of ...'

I smacked her hard around the face.

'You told them somebody was gonna be bumped. That's what you told them, didn't you?'

'Yeah,' she said, scared as hell.

'And who was gonna be bumped?' I demanded.

'Why ... er ... er ...'

I smacked her face again, hard. 'I was the guy that was gonna be bumped. Oh, you sure had it set sweet, sister. Phil was gonna bump me, the police were going to blast in, and you and Phil were gonna clear out and leave the rest of the boys to take the rap.'

'Hank, that's not right. I wouldn't wanna see you killed, honest I wouldn't.'

I carried on, ignoring her protests. 'And Phil double-crossed you, preferring to have the swag for himself, fixing it so it looked like I killed you, to put the cops off the scent.'

'That isn't true, Hank. I promise you it isn't true, it isn't true!' She screamed her protests and hammered on my chest, but I could see in her face that it was true, every word of it.

'I ought to kill you,' I said. I was thinking of Lola with a slug in her back, of Joel dangling by her wrists with the marks of the lash imprinted on her soft flesh. 'You rat,' I rasped. I seized her hair and strained her head back over the seat. She struggled, her body heaving while she tugged to get free. I fumbled in my pocket with one hand and got out my penknife. It had a sharp blade and I was flaming mad.

She was struggling like fury, scenting the cold animal anger inside me. She was desperate to get away. Then with one tug I sprawled her into my lap. I bent over her, pinioning her arms with my body and holding her head firm by her hair.

She went mad with pain and fear when I began to work with my knife. She shrieked like I never want to hear again. My hands got slippery with blood, and when I'd finished I was sweating and panting like a man that's been slinging coal at the coalface.

She huddled up in the other corner, sobbing and moaning and mopping up the blood that streamed down her face.

'Shut up, can't you?' I yelled suddenly, my nerves at breaking point. She still sobbed hysterically. I lit a cigarette and waited.

She stopped after a while. It was dark in the car.

'Hank,' she said, tearfully. 'What have you done to me?'

'You'll find out.'

'Tell me, Hank. Tell me, I must know.'

'I've branded you. I've branded you so that everyone you meet will know the truth. If anyone asks what that DC on your forehead stands for, you can tell them it means doublecrosser.'

There was stunned silence. Then, 'My God, my God!'

'Now get out,' I told her.

'What do you mean?' There was surprise and fear in her voice.

'Get out. Get out of this car.'

'Hank, you can't mean it. You're not leaving me.'

'I'm leaving you here.'

She grabbed hold of me by the arm. 'Hank, you can't leave me. Not now. Nobody will want me now. Don't you see? I'm yours now, nobody can take me away. I'm yours, Hank.'

'Out,' I said.

I got hold of the car door, swung it open and literally flung her into the road. She sprawled there as I slammed the door and started off.

I'd just got into second gear when I remembered the attaché case. I pulled up again and felt for it on the floor. It had come open, and in the dark I picked up the contents and thrust them back into the case.

I heard her shoes, clip-clopping on the road. I hadn't stopped my engine. I opened the door and threw the case out and slammed the door shut. But by this time she was round in front of me, hanging onto the radiator with her body in front of the nearside wheel. She looked a sight in the glare of my headlights, with her hair wildly dishevelled and the blood running down her face from the hideous cuts on her forehead.

I switched off the lights quick. I didn't want any passing motorist to get curious. Then I got out and went around to the front of the car. I took her by the throat. She leaned against me so I could feel her lovely limbs pressed against mine.

'Listen, you bitch. Don't get me madder than I am or I'll leave you here senseless.'

With that I gave her a thrust that sent her staggering away from me. The next moment she was back, clawing at me, pleading with words of passion and love. With one hand she ripped her blouse down to her waist so that she could press her soft flesh against me. Her arms wrapped around me, warm thighs pressed against mine, hot lips searched for mine. The blood rose up inside me, there was a mad, thrilling desire coursing through my veins, my resolve was growing weaker, swallowed up by desire. And then I saw a mind picture of Joel, her back torn by the lash, Phil folding up with a bullet in his guts, and the dead face of the big, bluff cop, all as a result of this girl, the female of the species, Garvin's sister.

I got one hand free and measured carefully. I held my punch, but it was enough to sprawl her in the grass gutter. Then I got in the car and started off as she began clawing to her feet. She made a wild snatch as I shot past, catching the door handle with her mitt. It didn't get her anywhere, except to pull her flat on her puss. The last I saw of her was a dim, shadowy figure standing in the middle of the road looking after me with an abandoned hopelessness.

I wondered if she'd have the nerve to stop a car with her puss cut up the way it was.

Half an hour later I stopped at a roadhouse. I went to the toilet first, locked myself in and cleaned Gwen's blood off my hands and clothes. Then I walked to the snack counter and grabbed myself some ham and eggs.

I didn't know what I was gonna do, how, when or why. I thought I might as well drive on as drive back. It would have been nice taking a long trip across America, seeing all those places I'd long wanted to see. But I just hadn't the dough.

I got back to my car, lit a fag and dropped the packet on the floor. I felt for it and found something bulky and unrecognisable. I picked it up and looked at it curiously by the light of my dashboard.

It was a thick wad of century notes, one that had fallen out of Gwen's attaché case. I counted them on the spot. There were exactly a hundred of them. Ten thousand dollars. I lit another cigarette and whistled through my teeth.

I haven't got many scruples. I hadn't stuck to that wad deliberately. Them being in my car was an accident.

But I sure wasn't gonna go back and find Gwen to hand them over.

I knew a fella what could find a method of making the best out of them.

I tucked the notes in my pocket, let in the clutch and drove on through the night, heading west across the states, whistling a quiet little melody and trying not to think about Joel.

ALSO AVAILABLE FROM TELOS PUBLISHING

CRIME

THE LONG, BIG KISS GOODBYE
by SCOTT MONTGOMERY
Hardboiled thrills as Jack Sharp gets involved with a
dame called Kitty.

MIKE RIPLEY

Titles in Mike Ripley's acclaimed 'Angel' series of comic
crime novels.

JUST ANOTHER ANGEL by MIKE RIPLEY
ANGEL TOUCH by MIKE RIPLEY
ANGEL HUNT by MIKE RIPLEY
ANGEL ON THE INSIDE by MIKE RIPLEY
ANGEL CONFIDENTIAL by MIKE RIPLEY
ANGEL CITY by MIKE RIPLEY
ANGELS IN ARMS by MIKE RIPLEY
FAMILY OF ANGELS by MIKE RIPLEY
BOOTLEGGED ANGEL by MIKE RIPLEY
THAT ANGEL LOOK by MIKE RIPLEY

HANK JANSON

Classic pulp crime thrillers from the 1940s and 1950s.

TORMENT by HANK JANSON
WOMEN HATE TILL DEATH by HANK JANSON

SOME LOOK BETTER DEAD by HANK JANSON
SKIRTS BRING ME SORROW by HANK JANSON
WHEN DAMES GET TOUGH by HANK JANSON
ACCUSED by HANK JANSON
KILLER by HANK JANSON
FRAILS CAN BE SO TOUGH by HANK JANSON
BROADS DON'T SCARE EASY by HANK JANSON
KILL HER IF YOU CAN by HANK JANSON
LILIES FOR MY LOVELY by HANK JANSON
BLONDE ON THE SPOT by HANK JANSON
THIS WOMAN IS DEATH by HANK JANSON
THE LADY HAS A SCAR by HANK JANSON

Non-fiction

THE TRIALS OF HANK JANSON by STEVE
HOLLAND

TELOS PUBLISHING
Email: orders@telos.co.uk
Web: www.telos.co.uk

To order copies of any Telos books, please visit our
website where there are full details of all titles and
facilities for worldwide credit card online ordering, as
well as occasional special offers.

33411262R00080

Made in the USA
Charleston, SC
13 September 2014